A Sticky Inheritance

Maple Syrup Mysteries Book 1

Emily James

Stronghold Books
ONTARIO, CANADA

Emily James
authoremilyjames@gmail.com
www.authoremilyjames.com

This is a work of fiction. I made it up. You are not in my book. I probably don't even know you. If you're confused about the difference between real life and fiction, you might want to call a counselor rather than a lawyer because names, characters, places, and incidents in this book are a product of my twisted imagination. Real locales and public names are sometimes used for atmospheric purposes. Any resemblance to actual people, living or dead, or to businesses, companies, events, and institutions is completely coincidental.

Book Layout ©2013 BookDesignTemplates
Cover Design by Deranged Doctor Designs

A Sticky Inheritance/Emily James. -- 1st ed.
ISBN 978-0-9920372-5-3

For my mom, without whom I wouldn't exist and my books wouldn't have titles.

It is hard to believe that a man is telling the truth when you know that you would lie if you were in his place.

—HENRY LOUIS MENCKEN

Chapter 1

When we got the call about my Uncle Stan's death and I decided to make the ten-hour drive to arrange his funeral since my parents refused, I hadn't counted on two things.

How much colder Lower Michigan was even in October than Northern Virginia, where I grew up.

And the tractors.

If it weren't for the freakish number of tractors using the roads up here, I wouldn't have been speeding, an hour behind schedule, and I certainly wouldn't have ended up stranded on the side of the road with a flat tire and a car that now sounded like it was trying to digest a stomach full of rocks. When the tractor had been coming toward me, taking up my half of the road as well as his, the logical thing to do seemed to be to swerve out of the way.

I hadn't realized at the time that the driver would move over at the last minute to let me safely by. I hadn't even known if he could see my little Acura from his perch. And who could have predicted that the gravel shoulder would be so soft, dragging me sideways into the edge of some farmer's field?

I squatted as well as I could in my pencil skirt and peered under the back end of my car, next to the flat tire. Rusty wire fencing wrapped around the other back wheel, and a wooden post had jammed itself up into the metal that connected the wheel to the rest of my car.

My car wasn't going anywhere. Not on its own, anyway.

I picked my way back to the more solid ground near the edge of the road and pulled my cell phone from my purse.

Before I could dial, a charcoal-gray pickup truck eased to a stop in front of me. The passenger-side window rolled down, and the man behind the wheel leaned toward it.

From what I could see, he looked to be a little older than me—maybe early to mid-thirties. His dark hair and vivid blue eyes reminded me a bit of a young Patrick Dempsey.

He smiled, revealing a dimple. "Need some help?"

I glanced back at my car. I did, but there wasn't anything he could do about it. "Unless you're carrying some spare parts and an industrial-size car jack in there, I think this is one for the tow truck."

A tell-tale heavy click signaled him unlocking the doors. "I can give you a lift into Fair Haven if you like. You'll be able to hire a tow truck from there."

I'm a regular at the women's self-defense classes at my gym—they're a great workout, not to mention that every woman should know how to protect herself—but even with that, climbing into a vehicle with a stranger in the middle of the boonies would be stupid. My mother raised me better than that.

Besides, what kind of person even offered anymore? I took a tiny step back and slid my right hand into my pocket where I'd shoved my keys. I wove them between my fingers just in case. "For all you know, I could be a serial killer."

His dimple grew. "Are you?"

"No." I couldn't keep from smiling back. He was charming. I'd give him that. But wasn't that what they said about all good psychopaths? "I could be lying in saying that, too, though."

He chuckled this time. "You're only about five minutes away by car, but it'll take you a lot longer to walk. Sure you don't want a lift?"

"That's what cell phones are for," I said, holding mine up. "I'll call Triple-A. But thanks anyway."

"It's hit and miss to get a signal out here." He shifted position and held up a wallet. "Would it make you feel better if I showed you my ID?"

I glanced at my phone. Two bars. It would be a crap shoot whether I could hold a signal long enough to call for help. Thunder growled in the distance, and a few drops of rain spattered my face. No way was I walking. My arms were already covered in goosebumps inside my coat. I'd probably freeze to death before I made it to town.

Still, I'd rather take a gamble on the cell signal than on the truthfulness of a man crazy enough to stop for a hitchhiker. "I'll be fine."

I backed one more step toward my car just in case he wouldn't take *no* for an answer and I had to hop inside. Not that I could drive away, but at least I could lock the doors.

He shrugged. "If you insist. Is it alright with you if I call a tow for you when I get back to town? Just in case."

A little worm of guilt wriggled around in my stomach. He probably was simply a Good Samaritan, but I was a criminal attorney, the daughter of two criminal attorneys. I knew too much about the evil in the world to risk it.

"I'd appreciate that." I reached for my door handle, then paused. "And thanks again for stopping."

He tipped his head, rolled up the window, and drove away.

I shivered and slid back into my car. The empty stretch of road suddenly felt a lot emptier.

For the next hour, I tried unsuccessfully to reach AAA or anyone who might be able to call a tow truck for that matter. Just when I was about to admit defeat, dig out a better pair of walking shoes, and brave the cold, a tow truck stopped next to my car.

If I ever saw my Good Samaritan again, I probably owed him a thank you—and an apology.

Fair Haven apparently had two options for car repairs—Quantum Mechanics and Fix-A-Dent. Since I had no idea how to choose between the two, I took the tow truck driver's advice and went with Quantum Mechanics. They were a little pricier, but better at fixing the "guts" of a car, as the driver put it. If I'd learned anything from my dad, it was that you get what you pay for, and given the sound my car was making, chances were good that post had punctured more than my tire.

I handed the signed papers across the counter. The bald man on the other side wore the greasy powder-blue jumpsuit that seemed to be the uniform for this place. His nametag read TONY.

Tony scooped up the papers and turned away. He smelled more like gasoline than a gas station did.

I worked on breathing through my mouth. I'm sensitive to almost every chemical imaginable. A headache was already blossoming behind my eyes, and I didn't need fumes adding to it. "Where do I get the keys for my loaner?"

He turned back from the filing cabinet. "We don't have loaners. Most people have a ride, or they just walk home."

Guess I'd be walking to my B&B...after the funeral home. I might need to dig better walking shoes out of my bag after all. "Could you tell me how to find Cavanaugh Funeral Home?"

"I wondered." The briskness had drained from his voice and he finally met my gaze instead of glancing nervously around like he'd rather be under a car than dealing with a person. There was a kindness there I hadn't expected. "It's off-season for tourists. Who are you here for?"

It was the longest string of words he'd spoken to me, and a lump formed in my throat. "Stan Dawes. My uncle. I'm here to make arrangements."

He shifted his weight from foot to foot. "We're planning on closing the shop for the funeral so everyone can go. Make sure you put an announcement in the paper once you have the time set."

"I will."

He cleared his throat and I could tell the touchy-feely part of the conversation was officially over. That was okay with me. If I was going to manage all of this on my own, I had to stay focused on the practical details and not on what I'd lost.

I readjusted my laptop bag, which was already cutting into my shoulder. "How did you say I get there?"

He pointed to the right. "Go that way when you leave here..."

His directions contained at least five streets named after trees. Directions had never been my strength, and it figured that my GPS system was integrated into my car.

I repeated the names over in order as I hauled my large, wheeled suitcase out the door.

The town screamed *tourist destination*. Not only were the streets unnaturally clean, but most of the clearly visible walls had been painted in such a way to be discussion pieces. Some of them made the buildings look like they'd been cracked open, giving you a peek inside at some upside down world, a jungle environment, or the inside of a pharaoh's tomb. Others sported mountain vistas that belonged in an art gallery.

By the time I passed Maple, Chestnut, and Pine Streets, I was lost. If Tony had given me directions based on the names of the stores, finding the funeral parlor would have been simple. Each store front carried a sign with a quirky name—Burnt Toast Café, The Sweet Tooth, Sew What Clothing and Shoes, A Salt and Battery (which from a glance in the window looked to be a restaurant specializing in fried fish), and Indiana Bones: Temple of Groom (with a giant smiling schnauzer face painted on the front window). The tourist board must have helped each business out with a name because there was no way everyone in this town could be that creative.

Cavanaugh Funeral Home should stand out from the normalcy of the name alone. Thankfully. If I'd gotten a call from a Deepest Holes Funeral Home, I would have drained my savings to fly Uncle Stan back to Virginia.

Unfortunately, I didn't see it anywhere. I dragged my bag into the nearest store, a hair salon called The Chop Shop.

The inside had 50s-style décor, right down to the checkerboard floor, alternating aqua and red chairs, and polka-dot dresses on the hair stylists. I could definitely see the appeal this town would have for vacationers, but it must be a little odd to live and work here.

I didn't mean to eavesdrop, but I couldn't help catching snatches of the local gossip. A brewer was in some kind of trouble with the law. Again. John Somebody's granddaughter was pregnant at sixteen. But that was no surprise since her mom was only a year older when she had the girl. And apparently there was an ongoing feud because Norma's neighbor's dog kept pooping on her lawn.

That was something else you didn't see in the city. Not the dog poop. We had plenty of that, even in an urban area. The gossip and sense of closeness. I barely knew my neighbors. I could be impregnated by an alien and no one would be the wiser.

"You're new," a little voice said.

I swiveled around. A seven-year-old boy sat cross-legged on the floor, surrounded by trucks. For a second, all I could see was myself at his age. My parents always seemed to have to work late, and so Uncle Stan's receptionist would pick me up at school and I'd play in a corner of his office until he finished with his last patient or my parents finished with their case preparation. I guess they figured I was safer around heart patients than I was around accused criminals.

The little boy flew a truck through the air like it was a plane. "You must be lost. We never get new people this time of year. The beaches are too cold, and the snow hasn't fallen yet."

I leaned my bag against one side of the loveseat in the waiting area and perched on the edge nearest where he played. "I am new. And I'm lost. I don't suppose you'd know how to find Cavanaugh Funeral Home, would you?"

He made a swooshing *vroom* noise. "My mom probably does. She knows everything. She even knows how to make Rice Krispy squares." Awe filled his voice.

I covered my mouth to hide a smile and glanced over my shoulder at the full seats. Four women filled the salon's chairs. Three of them were clearly the *come in every week for a wash and set* crowd. The fourth was a teenage girl with her hair covered in highlights foil. None of them looked like the right age for the boy's mother. "Does your mom work here?"

He nodded this time and crashed a plastic dump truck into the side of the sofa, complete with crashing sound effects.

"Can I help you?" a woman's voice said.

From her dark hair and eyes that matched the little boy's, this must be his mother.

The woman held out a hand. "I'm Liz. Were you looking for a walk-in spot? We should be able to take you if you're willing to wait five minutes."

I accepted her handshake, but motioned toward my suitcase. "Not today. I just got into town and I'm late for a meeting at the funeral home."

Liz gave me directions, using landmarks this time, and I backtracked two streets. Once I turned down the right road, the funeral home was easy to spot. The sign was clean and simple. The stone was a muted gray.

Walking backward, I dragged my suitcase up the stairs and inside, kicking myself that I'd never been good at packing light.

I smashed straight into a solid mass.

A man's voice grunted an *oomph*. Warm hands grabbed my upper arms and stopped me from toppling over and making a complete fool of myself.

Heat burned up my neck, and I righted myself. *A lawyer must always be poised and professional, Nicole.* My mother's familiar lecture played in my head even though she wasn't here to see me make a clumsy mess of something this time.

I smoothed my skirt and looked up at the man I'd nearly plowed down.

It was my Good Samaritan.

Chapter 2

"I guess I owe you two *thank you*s now," I blurted.

The dimple popped out in his cheek again. "Should I take that to mean the tow truck I sent reached you in time?"

Up close, I could see a smattering of gray in his dark hair and a day's growth of stubble on his chin, but the gray looked premature. Definitely in his late thirties. And much better looking than I'd thought. My stomach did a tumble of its own.

I straightened my already straight jacket and plastered what I hoped was an I'm-not-at-all-affected-by-how-good-looking-you-are smile on my face. I wasn't here to date. I was here to bury my uncle.

"It did. You were right that I couldn't get a cell signal. I might still be there without your help." I extended my hand. "Nicole Fitzhenry-Dawes."

His smile faded. "You're Stan's niece. I'm so sorry for your loss. He meant a lot to the people around here, you know."

I swallowed hard against the lump that wanted to form in my throat and lowered my hand. I suppose condolences were the expected reaction, but the more people who expressed grief over Uncle Stan's passing, the harder it was for me to hold it together. "Thank you. You knew him?"

"We volunteered for a lot of the same causes. I didn't realize who you were when I stopped earlier or I would have tried even harder to convince you to accept a ride. You don't sound like you're from Virginia."

I rolled my eyes. "Northern Virginia, on the outskirts of DC. We're accent-neutral."

He finally extended his hand. "Mark Cavanaugh."

It was my turn to leave his hand hanging. It took all my focus to keep my mouth from dropping open. "You're the funeral director?" I expected someone much older and less sexy.

He chuckled softly. "County medical examiner, actually."

Now I was confused. "Is it normal for the medical examiner to meet with the family of the deceased?"

"Huh?" His eyebrows drew down in a quizzical frown, then lifted. "Oh. No, I'm waiting for my brother, and he's been waiting for you. Cavanaugh Funeral Home is our family business, but my brother Grant took it over and I went to medical school."

"The joke around town," a voice nearly identical to Good Samaritan Mark's said from behind me, "is that if anyone will be found guilty of murder in Fair Haven, it'll be a Cavanaugh because we're the family that already deals in death."

I turned to face the new arrival, and I had to bite the inside of my cheek to keep from letting out a childish yelp. I looked back to Mark. He was still there. He hadn't teleported to the other side of me. The two men were identical. "Is this place like Stepford Husbands or something?"

The second Cavanaugh brother laughed, but it trickled away quickly, and Mark's smile looked tense. I got the feeling I'd swallowed my foot, I just didn't know how. The silence stretched a little too long.

The second Cavanaugh brother cleared his throat. "Sorry, no weird cloning or body-snatching experiments going on here. I'm Grant Cavanaugh, and I'm the one you're here to see."

I did shake Grant Cavanaugh's hand. Seeing them standing side by side, I could pick out a few small differences now. Grant didn't have Mark's dimple or his smattering of silver hairs. I did belatedly notice that both men wore wedding rings.

Grant swiped his arm in an arc. "My office is this way."

I leaned my suitcase against a wall. If someone wanted the heavy thing badly enough to steal it, I could replace anything in it. Better that than breaking myself by continuing to lug it around after me.

"Before we talk arrangements..." I shoved my hands in my pockets to keep from smoothing my jacket again. I was a big girl. I could handle this. Even alone. "I'd like to see my uncle, please."

"He hasn't been prepared, and the mortuary fridge isn't the place where you want to see him and say your good-byes. Why don't you wait until we have his body ready for viewing?"

He was probably right, but I needed to see my uncle. Since my parents got the call, I'd kept expecting someone to call back and say it'd been a mistake. They'd confused Uncle Stan with someone else. My rational mind knew that wasn't possible. People here knew him—had known him for well over ten years—but that last seed of hope wouldn't die, and I couldn't accept reality until I'd seen him. I didn't want to wait.

"I'm a criminal defense attorney. I've seen my share of crime scene photos. I promise you I can handle it."

A little white lie never hurt anyone, right? I was a defense attorney, but I'd never been the lead on a case, and I hadn't actually looked that closely at many crime scene photos. Blood and anything medical made me feel faint—only one of the many waving red flags that should have warned me I might be getting into the wrong profession.

Grant nodded slowly and led the way through a door marked STAFF ONLY. He lifted the handle on a heavy silver door inside. "Give me one minute."

He was back in less. He held the door open, and Mark followed me in. My legs felt like I was the one with rigor mortis, my knees locking and making each step awkward and heavy.

I silently cursed out my parents. I shouldn't have had to do this alone. No matter how angry my dad still was at Uncle Stan, they'd been brothers.

I stopped five feet back from the metal table where...my legs didn't seem to want to...

I sucked deep breaths in through my nose and out through my mouth. Hold it together, Nik. You're a thirty-year-old woman. You're not a little girl.

I inched the rest of the way until I stood close enough to touch him. The color in his face was wrong, a strange pasty blue like someone dropped a robin's egg in bleach. He'd aged since I'd seen him last, his hair thinner and the wrinkles around his jowls more pronounced, which I should have expected, since the last day we were together was the week before my sixteenth birthday. The last day I hugged him.

I blinked hard. I wasn't going to cry here, in front of strangers. I could cry later.

Pressure built in my chest and behind my eyes, and I couldn't help it. The tears came hard enough that I gulped in air and hiccupped it out. He'd been my only uncle and as much a father to me as my dad. I hadn't spoken to my dad for nearly a month after he banned Uncle Stan from trying to contact any of us unless it was to tell us he'd come to his senses. I'd been grounded for almost that long when Dad found the long distance charge on our phone bill the time I broke the rules and called Uncle Stan here in Fair Haven.

It was an embarrassingly long time before I could get control of my tears. I wiped my eyes with the back of my sleeve, leaving a mascara smear on the dry-clean-only wool. What kind of an idiot doesn't buy herself waterproof mascara for a funeral? "Sorry. I think some part of me didn't believe he was actually dead."

"There's nothing to apologize for. It's a normal reaction." Mark handed me a wrinkled brown napkin that looked like it'd come from a fast food restaurant. "It's all I could find in my pockets."

Grant's face was red all the way to the tips of his ears. "We have tissues all over the place, but not in the fridge. You looked like you'd be okay."

My breakdown clearly rattled him enough to shake the professional funeral director veneer. I waved my hand in my best not-your-fault gesture and tried to dab my runny nose in as ladylike a manner as possible. It wasn't working. I gave an internal shrug and blew my nose into the napkin. The honk was so loud I could sense my mother cringing six hundred miles away.

But who really cared if they saw me doing something as disgusting as blowing my nose? They were both married, and it's not like they were even potential clients. I was only here for a week or so to settle the funeral details and deal with Uncle Stan's estate. After that, I'd be back to Virginia. And besides, knowing I'd blown my nose in front of them should make me embarrassed enough to overlook the fact that both brothers belonged in some sort of male pin-up calendar.

I shoved the slimy napkin into my pocket and swallowed down a final hiccup. "How did he die?"

Grant and Mark exchanged a glance. It was more of a silent conversation really, one jutting his chin and the other raising his eyebrows just a hair and giving an almost imperceptible shake of his head. Had I not been trained to observe every detail, I might have missed it all.

Finally Mark sighed. "Didn't the officer who contacted you explain the situation?"

I hadn't spoken to the officer. My dad was officially next of kin, so whoever gave the notification called my parents' house. I'd been there for supper, otherwise they might not have even told me Uncle Stan was dead. But I didn't want to try to explain my family dynamics to either of these men. They clearly had a strong bond, and it would only cast a pall over Uncle Stan's memory to wave about all the family skeletons in their dirty underwear.

"My parents didn't share the details with me, only that he'd died." My voice cracked again on the last word and I drew in a deep breath, holding it until I felt steady again.

Mark's eyes had taken on that pitying look that people got when they had to break bad news. My heartbeat grew so loud in my ears that it threatened to drown out everything else.

He twisted his wedding ring around on his finger. "Stan's autopsy showed a high alcohol level in his blood stream and an overdose of his heart medication. It wasn't clear whether the overdose was accidental or suicide."

Chapter 3

A shiver rolled over me that had nothing to do with the temperature in the fridge. Thirteen years ago, Uncle Stan was diagnosed with a heart condition. I'd assumed that's what killed him. Now they were saying his death was by his own hand, maybe intentionally. "That's not possible."

"I know how upsetting it can be to hear a loved one might have taken their own life." Mark had stopped twisting his ring, and he met my gaze now. "But I performed the autopsy myself. And I double-checked because I knew Stan, and I didn't think it fit, either. The results are sound."

The results might be, but their conclusions weren't. "My uncle doesn't...didn't drink. At all. Ever. You performed the autopsy, so you must have read his medical records by now." I tapped the spot over my own heart with two fingers. "His heart condition was alcoholic cardiomyopathy."

"Which is caused by years of heavy drinking."

Mark's voice was too soft and patient. He probably didn't mean it to be, but it bordered on patronizing. Made me want to stomp on his foot.

Instead, I straightened my shoulders and glared at him. "He's been sober since his diagnosis. He used to be one of the most highly regarded cardiologists in the country. He wouldn't have taken the risk of drinking again. Not with his condition and not with the medication he was on."

He was the reason I was an anomaly among my generation. I hadn't touched a drop of alcohol since the night he'd caught my friends and me with a bottle of wine we'd swiped from my dad's collection. He'd put the fear into me that I'd let future stress and peer pressure push me into drinking more than was healthy. He'd made me promise not to risk my life the way he'd risked his. I was fifteen. Two weeks later, he announced he was quitting his practice and buying a farm here in Fair Haven.

Mark frowned. "He was a doctor?"

I planted my hands on my hips in my best impression of my mom's don't-mess-with-me pose. "One of the very best. He'd travel all over giving lectures. Your results might be right, but they don't make sense."

"People do slip," Grant said. "If he happened to be depressed, maybe he went back to what comforted him in the past."

Mark rubbed the back of his pointer finger against his lips and gave a grudging nod.

Now I wanted to stomp on Grant's foot, too. I'd almost won Mark over as my ally. And I'd need an ally if I was going to convince the powers that be in this town to reopen the investigation into Uncle Stan's death. I was an outsider here.

I chewed on my bottom lip. Was I really going to argue that his death was suspicious, though? The Cavanaughs wouldn't be the only ones to think I was crazy or unreasonable. Yet the only other alternative was to accept that the man I'd hero worshipped most of my life wasn't at all who I thought he was. The uncle I knew never would have killed himself or made such a foolish mistake.

"Did he seem depressed to either of you? Did any of his friends seem worried about him?"

"Nicole." Mark took my elbow and led me out of the fridge. "Depression isn't always easy to spot or understand, even when you're close to someone. How long has it been since you've seen your uncle?"

Ouch. He probably well knew thanks to small-town gossip that this was my first visit to Fair Haven and that Uncle Stan never went back to Virginia after he settled here. It wasn't that I hadn't wanted to see him again. At first I couldn't because of my parents, but then there'd been college, then law school and clerking in the summers.

That didn't mean, though, that I'd lost touch with him. Since I moved out on my own, we'd either talked or emailed every week.

I yanked my phone out of my purse and brought up my email account. I scrolled through until I found what I was looking for and pressed it. I highlighted a section and shoved my phone at Mark. "Read this."

Hopefully he wasn't nosy enough to read the text surrounding it. The email I'd pulled up was Uncle Stan's reply a week ago to an email I'd sent telling him I wasn't sure I wanted to be a lawyer anymore and expressing my fears over what would happen if I decided to quit. Uncle Stan was the only one who could understand.

Everyone in my family for over a hundred years back on both sides had been either a doctor or a lawyer. As the daughter of two lawyers, no one ever asked me what I wanted to be when I grew up. Obviously, I'd be a lawyer. And growing up on shows like *Matlock*, I thought being a defense attorney would be the best job ever. I'd get to run around solving puzzles, uncovering clues, and proving that my client was really innocent. Most of the time, I'd even identify the actual bad guy for the police.

Real life didn't quite meet my expectations. Most of the people my parents defend are guilty. I'd developed insomnia worrying about the criminals we were trying to set free or win the shortest possible sentence for.

For a while, I thought I could simply switch to being a prosecutor once I had a few years' experience, but they didn't solve cases, either. They took the evidence given to them by the police and had to decide whether there was enough of it to bring charges. Their lives were more about debating and weighing the odds than about deduction and investigating. I'm good one on one, but it turns out I didn't inherit the public speaking gene. My tendency to botch my opening and closing statements was the reason I'd never been given the lead on a case.

And heaven knows I'm not cut out to be a cop. I'd probably accidentally shoot myself in the foot on the first day.

The bottom line was that what I'd loved about being a lawyer, what I'd dreamed about, was something lawyers didn't actually get to do. That's what I told Uncle Stan in my email, along with the fear of what my parents' reaction would be. They'd shunned Uncle Stan because he gave up his successful life to be a "hick farmer," as my dad called it. I still remembered them arguing about Uncle Stan throwing away his talent.

I knew exactly what would happen if I gave up practicing law.

Uncle Stan wrote back that living life miserable and afraid was no life at all. He'd loved his patients, loved his job, but it still wasn't right for him. The stress and long hours, the lives that hung on his decisions, had sucked all the joy out of his life until he'd almost drunk himself into an early grave. The best decision he ever made was moving to Fair Haven and buying Sugarwood. He'd never been happier or more content.

I examined Mark's face as he read. His expression didn't give anything away.

He handed the phone back to me. "It could have still been accidental. Maybe he took a double dose by accident because he'd been drinking."

Now he sounded more like he felt the need to raise every possible objection than that he actually believed what he was arguing for. "Maybe, but I don't think so. If we could get into his house, I could at least examine his pill box and look around for any alcohol or empty bottles or cans. Did the police check those things?"

"I couldn't say for sure. I turn in my report, but I'm not involved in any other part of their investigations. If you'd like, I'll take you to see the chief of police, and you can ask him any questions you have. Would that set your mind at ease?"

This time I wouldn't turn down his offer of a ride. However far away the chief's office was, it was too far. My feet were already aching, and I swear my suitcase was mocking me. "Yes, please. I'd appreciate that."

"Mark?" Grant said.

We both turned in his direction.

His face was hard. "A word."

Mark followed him to the other side of the room, next to the doors that I guessed led into the visitation rooms based on the pedestals next to each door for guest books.

"What do you think you're doing?" Grant asked, his words almost a hiss.

"She raises enough good questions that I want some answers. It's probably nothing, but Stan was too good a man for me not to at least follow up on this."

It was strange watching twins arguing, like seeing a person fight with their reflection in a mirror.

Grant crossed his arms over his chest. "You don't need to be involved any more than you already are in another suicide."

I didn't mean to eavesdrop, but the sound in here carried and it would look quite odd if I stuck my fingers into my ears. I turned my back to them to give the impression of privacy at least.

"I'm fine," Mark said. "This isn't the same."

I stole a peek over my shoulder.

Mark walked a little ways away, dialing a number as he went. "Carl? It's Mark. Do you have a few minutes? I'd like to bring Stan's niece by..."

They might not have completely believed me yet, but I knew my Uncle Stan. This wasn't a mistake. It wasn't an accident. It wasn't suicide.

It was murder.

Chapter 4

Mark returned to where I was waiting, his phone already back in his pocket. "I told him everything you said. He can't get away tonight, and he asked that we don't go poking around—"

I raised an eyebrow at him.

He held up his hands. "His words, not mine. That we don't go poking around without him. If there is evidence of something, he wants to properly document it before we touch it. Since the scene's already been released, nothing we find will be admissible, but they could still use it to point them in the right direction for investigating."

Okay, that made sense. Evidence could easily be accidentally contaminated, lost, or muddled. "Fair enough."

"You weren't planning on staying there tonight, were you?"

In my dead uncle's house? No thanks. "I booked a room at The Sunburnt Arms."

The name had seemed strange to me when I reserved my room, but it was the only place open in the off-season. According to the lady I spoke with, the other bed and breakfasts wouldn't open up again until after the first big snowfall or for the Christmas season, whichever came first. Now that I'd seen more of Fair Haven, The Sunburnt Arms seemed to be a perfect fit name-wise.

I shot my giant suitcase—I swear it'd gained another ten pounds of girth since I'd left it leaning against the wall—another quick glare. "Could you tell me how to get there from here? Preferably with landmarks rather than street names."

Mark grabbed hold of my suitcase handle and pulled it toward the door as if it weighed no more than a pair of shoes. "It's too far for you to walk. I'll give you a lift."

I followed him out to the same charcoal-gray pickup he'd been driving before. I had to do an awkward hop and slide to climb in. Clearly whoever designed trucks didn't expect women in narrow skirts to be riding in them.

My cheeks burned and I peeked over to where Mark was. He either hadn't noticed my graceless entry or he was too much of a gentleman to show it.

He tossed my suitcase into the truck bed and climbed in. "I'll have to pick you up tomorrow morning as well. Sugarwood is on the opposite end of town from The Sunburnt Arms." He flashed me that gorgeous dimple again. "Assuming you don't mind me tagging along. If someone did harm your uncle, I'd like to know."

If it wasn't for the wedding ring, I would have almost thought he was flirting with me. And I was more grateful to him than I could say for giving me a moment of normal and a reason to smile.

The Sunburnt Arms turned out to be a "painted lady," a large Victorian-style home decked out in different colors to set off the architecture. This one's colors were more tastefully done than some of the ones I'd seen—a muted dusty rose offset with pale blue, white trim around the windows and partial wrap-around porch, and a slate-gray roof. I couldn't see them from the road, but the website had mentioned gazebos out back and a dock down at the water with plenty of comfy chairs for lounging. It would have been a restful place to visit under different circumstances.

Mark brought my suitcase right up to the entrance door for me and tipped an imaginary hat. "I'll be back at 8:15 tomorrow."

I threw a goofy little curtsy in return, then mentally kicked myself all the way to the front desk. What would my mother say? Of course, she wasn't here to see me, so maybe it served her right if I let my silly side out a bit. I'd have plenty of time to rein it back in once I returned to Virginia and my regular life.

Even though we arrived five minutes early, a police cruiser was already waiting for us in front of Uncle Stan's house when we pulled up. A tall, lean man in uniform leaned against the hood. Despite what I considered to be the cold morning air, he wasn't wearing a jacket. How anyone survived a winter here when fall already felt frigid was beyond me.

I hopped out of Mark's truck with more ease than I'd climbed in the day before. I'd opted for a dark pair of jeans, a white blouse, and flats this morning.

The uniformed man pushed off his car and met us halfway to the house. He had a long stride and a way of swinging his arms when he moved that reminded me a bit of a gorilla.

"I'm Chief Carl Wilson. And you must be Ms. Fritzhenry-Dawes."

He said my last name with that little curl to his lip that I'd noticed some people get in reaction to a hyphenated last name. Like they think it means I'm illegitimate or something. All it really meant was that my mother kept her last name for career reasons, and when I was born, my parents felt the only fair thing was to give me both last names. "I prefer Nicole."

He shook my hand and then Mark's, which made it clear to me that the two men had a strictly professional relationship rather than a personal one. They probably didn't meet for beers after work. Still, from the fact that the chief was willing to even come out here this morning and humor me, I had to believe it was a professional relationship built on mutual respect.

Chief Wilson unlocked the front door to the house. Whatever type of home I'd pictured Uncle Stan living in over the years, this wasn't it. The lower level was built out of dark gray stone, and the upper half, including the balcony overlooking the maple-filled bush behind, was rich red wood, like a luxury log cabin.

He stepped aside and held the door open. "I checked with Russ. He and I have the only keys that he knows of, and no one's been inside since the ambulance took Stan's body away." He glanced at me and flinched slightly as if realizing belatedly I might not want to hear about my uncle's body.

I pretended I hadn't noticed and went inside. The house was decorated with the same plain, comfortable-looking furniture that Uncle Stan preferred even back in Virginia.

For some reason, I always expected a house where someone died to smell different. It didn't. The house smelled like Uncle Stan, like coffee and peppermints.

My chest hollowed out. I didn't want to be here. Not like this. I should have found the time to visit him when he was still alive and the courage to visit him no matter what my parents would think. It shouldn't have taken him dying to get me up here.

A hand brushed my shoulder and I jumped.

"You okay?" Mark whispered.

I swallowed to moisten my suddenly dry throat and keep my voice from cracking and giving me away. "Of course. Why?"

"You had that same look on your face as you did yesterday, before..." He shifted his weight and patted his pocket. "I brought tissues this time in case you need them."

Crap. I dropped my gaze, blinking rapidly. He was going to make me cry from his thoughtfulness if he wasn't careful. "I'll check the drawers in his bedside table. That's where he used to keep his pill box."

"Just don't touch it if you do find it." Chief Wilson held up a camera. "Since you're sure Stan couldn't have possibly died the way we think he did, we're going to document everything just in case it turns out you're right."

I found the stairs and headed up. The staircase and all the inside walls upstairs were made of the same rich red wood as outside. A log cabin seemed somehow fitting for a man who'd owned a sugar bush, and yet he'd still managed to find himself a home with a certain elegance.

I opened the few doors upstairs until I stumbled upon the master bedroom. The bed was made, and three books he'd never finish reading rested on the bedside table. I knew they had to be unfinished. A book stayed on the shelf until he was ready to read it and it went back on the shelf as soon as he finished. Everything had its place in his home. I couldn't imagine living here had changed that.

Even though I was supposed to be looking for the pill box, I couldn't keep away from the books. We'd often choose a novel to read "together." Usually a mystery so we could see who would guess the murderer first.

I turned the books so I could read the spines. A leather-bound copy of the Bible with the gold lettering almost worn off. I set it aside. A medical thriller, based on the picture on the cover. He'd dog-eared a page a third of the way through. It joined the Bible on the bed.

The bottom book was wider and heavier than the first two. It looked like one of Uncle Stan's old reference texts from back when he was still practicing medicine. Not exactly what I'd call light bedroom reading.

He'd folded down a page corner in this one as well, something I knew from my years hanging around his office that he didn't normally do with his reference books. He'd once told me that if he marked those pages they'd all eventually be turned down and he'd never find anything. Maybe that didn't matter anymore since he wasn't actively using them. This book was probably well out of date.

I flipped the manual open to the page he'd marked. It was a section about caffeine's negative interactions with the heart. Or at least that's as much as I could understand of it. I only spoke one second language, and it was legalese, not medical jargon.

I opened the drawer. As I expected, Uncle Stan's pill box lay inside. I took a pen from my purse and poked the pill box around enough so I could see what days were empty and what days were full. I counted back. He'd taken his regular dose the day he died. That lent a little credence to my theory at least. He wouldn't have accidentally taken a dose even drunk because he had his pill box, and wouldn't a man who was going to kill himself simply overdose from his prescription bottle rather than bothering to first take the dose he'd measured out for himself?

I left the drawer open but put the books back where I found them in case Chief Wilson would be angry I touched them even though they weren't evidence of any kind.

I jogged back down the stairs. "I found his pill box and..."

Mark and Chief Wilson stood in front of the open refrigerator door, photographing something inside.

My stomach dipped and I crept toward them. A six-pack of beer bottles sat in Uncle Stan's fridge. I didn't recognize the brand. The case was green and brown, with the words *Beaver Tail Brew* emblazoned across the side.

Only two beers were missing.

My breath came out in a whoosh I hadn't realized I'd been holding. Two beers weren't enough to make a man drunk. Two beers certainly weren't enough to raise his blood alcohol levels to what Mark had told me they were on our ride to my B&B last night.

"I'll take these in as evidence," Chief Wilson said, "but it seems to confirm our original conclusions."

"His pill box doesn't," I said. "I left the drawer open and the box inside."

Mark gave a start and Chief Wilson pivoted around on his heel. I guess they hadn't heard me come in.

"Besides," I pointed to the six-pack, "that's not enough alcohol to prove anything."

Why did he have it in his house at all though? a little voice in the back of my mind whispered. If Uncle Stan never drank, the way I'd believed and insisted, his house should have been alcohol-free.

Chief Wilson snapped on a pair of latex gloves. "It's not. That's why we're going to check his garbage can next for empties."

We all trundled out the back to the black plastic trash can that stood nearly as tall as I did. Mark donned gloves as well and tipped the can while Chief Wilson poked around inside.

He pulled his arm back out, his hand clasped around the handle of another six-pack of empties.

No. I refused to accept it. It didn't make sense with what I knew and with what the pill box suggested.

My brain immediately started to spin with possible explanations. As a defense attorney, it was part of my job to come up with alternate reasons for how seemingly damning evidence could have shown up where it had. It was one of the few parts of being a lawyer I was good at. That training and natural *but/if* ability wasn't something I could have turned off, even if I wanted to. Right now, I definitely didn't want to. "Whoever killed my uncle could have planted the beer and the empties."

A scowl flickered across Chief Wilson's face, then was gone. Even Mark's expression was more skeptical than I was comfortable with.

I held up a hand. "Just listen for a minute." The little gears in my brain were clicking things into place, but I needed a second to sort it all out. "Why are all the empty bottles still in the case in the trash can, but there weren't empty bottles in the fifth and sixth spots in the fridge. Did you find them in the trash can inside?"

Chief Wilson set the six-pack aside and crossed his arms, but Mark shook his head.

"Then where did they go? And why put these back so meticulously, especially if he was drunk by the time he finished? Why put them out here at all if he planned to kill himself?"

"She makes some good points," Mark said.

Chief Wilson sighed. "I said I'd take this all in and test it, but you know better than anyone how hard it is to accept that someone you loved killed themselves. That can cause you to see bad guys where there aren't any."

Mark's face closed down, all expression gone. "Low blow, Carl."

"I'm just saying, don't get her hopes up."

I hated feeling like I was missing something, but now wasn't the time to ask either of them what Chief Wilson meant by that comment. I'd seen enough unwilling witnesses try to throw up smoke screens that I could recognize it when it happened. Chief Wilson didn't want us calling into question the county's determination about the cause of Uncle Stan's death. But finding out the truth mattered to me more than sparing the ego of a small-town police chief.

"It might be that you're correct," Mark said before I could speak, "but there are enough questions here that it warrants further investigation." His voice had a hard edge to it.

Chief Wilson dipped his head. "I'm not saying there aren't. I'm gonna take this all in and have the techs go over it." He met and held Mark's gaze. "But I'm hoping you're both wrong, because I'd much rather grieve for a good man who took his own life than have the town up in a panic over a murderer on the loose."

Chapter 5

Finishing arrangements at the funeral home had been easier than I expected. According to Grant, Uncle Stan had made most of the arrangements and paid in advance because of his heart condition. We scheduled a single viewing for the next day and the funeral for the day after.

Since the arrangements hadn't taken as long as I expected, I stopped in at the newspaper office to place an announcement (I'd looked up the address the night before and drew myself a map) on my way to Uncle Stan's lawyer.

My parents hadn't exactly encouraged my trip up here, so I had no more time than any other employee on bereavement leave would before I needed to return to work. Today was Thursday, and I was expected back in the office by next Wednesday. That meant I needed to settle everything as quickly as possible.

Settling everything now included making sure Chief Wilson would continue investigating Uncle Stan's death after I was gone. Chief Wilson didn't know it yet, but I'd be dropping by for a visit if I finished with the lawyer in time. I might not have inherited my parents' natural confidence and poise, but I did inherit their tenacity—Uncle Stan always called it stubbornness.

The lawyer's office was as tastefully and discreetly named as the funeral home. They'd stenciled MCCLANAHAN & ASSOCIATES on their front window in burgundy. Maybe the common denominator was the businesses that catered to the locals didn't need to be flashy.

One of those cute little front door bells jingled as I entered.

The receptionist behind the desk had dyed blonde hair, blue eyes, and a long, hooked nose like the goblins in *Harry Potter*. It didn't fit with the rest of her, which had clearly been tucked and Botoxed so that the doctor who delivered her wouldn't recognize anything. I couldn't imagine why she'd leave a nose like that unless she ran out of money. She'd be almost pretty without that nose...in a creation-of-Dr. Frankenstein kind of way.

A placard on the desk declared her *Ashley Jenkins, Receptionist.*

She looked down at me over the top of the square, black-rimmed, designer glasses perched on top of that nose. "May I help you?"

Her tone said *what do* you *want?* She would have lasted exactly one day in my parents' office.

I gave her my name, and Tom McClanahan came out to greet me. He looked exactly like his picture on their website—neatly trimmed goatee, wire-rimmed glasses, and an angular face.

What I hadn't been able to tell from the website photo was that he was almost my height. At only five foot five inches, I wasn't accustomed to looking men straight in the face. It made me strangely uncomfortable.

He ushered me into the office and closed the door solidly behind us. "Please take a seat, Ms. Fitzhenry-Dawes."

He didn't sneer my hyphenated last name, so I had to give him points for that.

Instead of settling in behind his desk, he balanced on the edge. I slid my chair back a bit so I could see him better. At least now his head was higher than mine, so that was a relief.

"This is an awkward situation." He steepled his fingers. "Many people were skeptical when your uncle purchased Sugarwood, but over the years he's proven to be a valuable member of this community."

I nodded as if I understood where he was going with this even though I didn't. How could the contents of a will be an awkward situation? Uncle Stan didn't have a lot of family, and my parents certainly weren't in need of his money, nor did they want it. If Uncle Stan left everything to charity, it would probably actually be simpler. Though I suppose not every relative would feel that way, so perhaps that's why Tom McClanahan felt the need to preface the reading of the will.

He leaned a little farther forward, and I had to clamp my hands around the arms of my chair to keep from instinctively reaching out to prevent him from toppling over.

"You do understand, don't you?" he said. "When you have so many tourists passing through each year, a community actually becomes tighter and more suspicious of strangers rather than more open and accepting of them."

I hadn't seen that in the Cavanaugh brothers, but perhaps that explained Ashley's attitude and the fact that the tow truck driver had only answered direct questions on the drive here.

Tom McClanahan was still talking. "Many of the families here depend on your uncle's sugar bush for their livelihood. I cautioned your uncle against making the choices he made in his will."

A lightbulb went on in my head. "I don't know the contents of my uncle's will, Mr. McClanahan."

His mouth formed into an O shape. "I'd assumed he'd discussed it with you."

"I'm afraid not."

Which was yet another piece of evidence that Uncle Stan hadn't killed himself. He didn't like loose ends. If there was something in his will that I should have been aware of before he died, he would have let me know.

Tom McClanahan gave a slow nod. "I see." He hopped down off the edge of his desk, moved around back, and drew a file from his filing cabinet. He sank into his chair, putting him below eye level again. "Well, other than a donation to his church, your uncle bequeathed all his worldly possessions to you. That includes his car, his home, the contents of his bank account, his investments, and all the land and equipment associated with Sugarwood."

I leaned back in my chair. I felt a little dizzy. I certainly hadn't expected that. I'd come down here with instructions from my parents to "get rid of everything." They'd assumed, as had I, that they'd be Uncle Stan's beneficiaries.

I had no idea what to do with a farm. "You don't have to worry. I won't be keeping the property. I'll find a buyer for it."

"That's what I was afraid of." He let out a sigh that seemed too large for such a small man. "Most of the people around here won't be able to afford what your uncle's property is worth, and selling it to an outside entity could be devastating. Sugarwood needs an owner who will be here and who understands the ebb and flow of a tourist town."

I didn't know what to say to that. I guess I could sell it at a loss to a local. I hadn't expected to inherit anything, so it wasn't like I'd been counting on the income from it.

"Your uncle's stated wish," Tom McClanahan said, "was for you to take over Sugarwood. He said it was the place he found himself and that you might need to do the same."

The place he found himself. It sounded a bit new-agey for my church-going uncle, but I got the message. If I wanted to quit my job and figure out what I wanted from my life rather than what my parents wanted, he'd given me the place to do it. "Was this a recent change to his will?"

"Only last month. That's why I remember it so well."

Last month was when I first told Uncle Stan I wasn't sure I wanted to be a lawyer anymore, shortly after my disastrous situation with my ex-boyfriend and my first-ever investigation.

I rubbed my hands up and down my jeans. I wasn't sure I wanted to be a lawyer anymore, but I also wasn't sure I wanted to be a farmer, either. Or a business owner. Or to leave the city for a small tourist town in Michigan.

Then again, I couldn't deny the appeal of living in a less complicated place. Uncle Stan made Fair Haven sound like the Garden of Eden.

I stood up. "Thank you. You're executor, correct? So you'll be handling everything to settle the estate?"

He jumped to his feet and followed me to the door. "I'll contact you when there's any paperwork to sign or decisions that need to be made."

I must have said goodbye and left the office, but the next thing I clearly remember, I was walking down the street. I probably should have asked him more questions about the specifics of what I'd inherited, but I could call back later, when I'd had time to come to terms with what this meant.

I changed directions to head for the chief's office. Technically speaking, if Uncle Stan's death was reopened and became an active investigation, Chief Wilson shouldn't tell me any specifics about the case. But I'd frustrated him enough with my mosquito-like questions yesterday that if I showed up in his office, he might tell me a little something simply to get rid of me.

Thankfully, the chief's office was also on the way back to my B&B. With all this walking, I didn't even need a workout.

I gave my name at the desk and took a seat on the backless metal bench against one wall. I appeared to be the only non-employee in the place, a testament to how quiet this town was, at least in the off-season. Crime probably skyrocketed when tourists flooded back in.

Even with my jacket still on, the station felt nippy. I swear, people who were raised here must be naturally hot-blooded. If I decided to stay, I'd have to face a Michigan winter.

I shivered. That was definitely one point in favor of going back home.

Chief Wilson must have hoped that if he kept me waiting long enough I'd give up. It was a good half hour before someone escorted me back to his office.

"How can I help you today?" he said as soon as the door closed behind me.

I'd never heard anyone actually sigh words before, but he managed it somehow.

I planted myself squarely in the chair in front of his desk and crossed my legs, making sure to show him I was willing to stay as long as it took to accomplish my mission. "I wanted to check in on the results from the beer bottles we discovered yesterday. Were there any fingerprints? Or DNA?"

Not subtle perhaps, but whatever Chief Wilson's other flaws might be, he didn't strike me as a stupid man. If I tried to trick him into answering my questions, he'd figure out immediately what I was doing.

He speared me with a flat gaze. "You're an attorney, aren't you? You know I can't discuss details with you."

So this was once again an open investigation. I did a little fist pump in my mind. "You can at least tell me if the results pointed to a suspect or not. You'd tell a reporter that."

"We have no suspects at present."

The one question I really wanted an answer to was one he might not budge on. It walked a gray line. "Were Uncle Stan's prints on the bottles?"

He pursed his lips. I'd bet my next coffee fix that he was debating with himself about whether it was better to shut me up by giving me a nibble of information or to hold strong and keep my nosy self out of it entirely.

He pressed his hands palm-down onto his desk. "The bottles were clean of prints."

I rocked back in my chair. That resolved any lingering doubts I might have had. And obviously it'd wiped away Chief Wilson's doubts as well since they'd reopened the investigation. No one who was so drunk he accidentally overdosed would wipe off his beer bottles. Neither would a man about to kill himself. Someone had forced Uncle Stan to drink that beer and had then wiped the bottles clean.

Chief Wilson raised his pointer finger and targeted it at me. "You get one more question before I kick you out of here, so you'd better make it good. I'm already going to be working late tonight."

Despite what the chief might think of me, I wasn't curious for the sake of being curious. All I cared about was that Uncle Stan received justice. Whoever hurt him deserved to pay. "What's the police department going to do next to make sure whoever did this is caught?"

Chief Wilson rubbed a hand over his scalp. His thinning hair stood on end, and for a minute, the chief persona melted away and all I saw was a very tired middle-aged man.

My stomach twisted a little. I shouldn't have given him as hard a time as I had. He wasn't my enemy. He wasn't the bad guy. He was just a man trying to do his job.

He leaned back in his chair. "I'll be honest with you, Ms. Fitzhenry-Dawes."

"Nicole."

"Right. Nicole." He almost smiled at me. It was uncanny. "The circumstances of your uncle's death mean we know it wasn't a random crime, but we have no leads and no idea who could have wanted him dead. Stan was respected and well-liked. He'd done more for this town than some people who'd lived here their whole lives. The only person who might have stood to benefit from his death was whoever inherited his estate. I plan to speak with his lawyer tomorrow about the contents of his will."

That would be a dead end. "I can save you some time there. I'm his sole heir."

"Then unless you want to confess to his murder," Chief Wilson shook his head and shrugged, "we have nowhere to go from here. We'll keep the case open on the chance anything turns up, but I'm afraid this one will likely go cold. We simply don't have enough to go on."

Chapter 6

All I could think about while waiting for Uncle Stan's funeral to start was how my dad always insisted that the perfect crime didn't exist. There was always something the perpetrator missed. My dad had been instructing me from a defense perspective, of course, training me to think ahead about what could have been missed and how I could explain it away should the prosecution find it. A good defense attorney was always one step ahead, he said.

In this case, though, it meant some trail had to exist that I could follow back to Uncle Stan's killer if I wanted to stay in Fair Haven and hunt for it. Chief Wilson made it clear two days ago that they didn't have enough evidence to call in outside help, and he didn't have the manpower to "go poking at rocks just to see what might crawl out." Based on a brief assessment of the town, I couldn't see where else he needed those men, but the last thing I wanted to be was a self-righteous city girl. I had to allow that a tourist town probably came with unique issues that local law enforcement worked hard to keep invisible.

I stood along with everyone else for the first hymn, then Uncle Stan's pastor gave a eulogy that focused more on Uncle Stan's faith than on his life—apparently at the request of my uncle himself. Even though I wasn't a churchgoer, it was comforting to think that Uncle Stan was happy now. If I stayed in Fair Haven, I might even consider attending his church on Sundays. I'd always kind of tuned Uncle Stan out before when he tried to talk to me about his church and his beliefs, but he was one of the most intelligent men I'd ever known, and he clearly thought there was something there worth listening to.

After the pastor finished, he opened the podium up to anyone who wanted to share a story about Uncle Stan. It was something Mark and Grant both suggested I allow. They said it helped people work through their grief if they could talk about the person they'd lost.

Story after story about Uncle Stan giving up his Saturday to help someone move, starting a fund to support a family whose child had leukemia, and basically being one of the best men I'd ever known continued until my heart hurt so much I was afraid I might be having a heart attack myself. How could the police department not drop everything else to figure out who'd killed him?

How could I leave when I might be the only person willing to actively hunt for his killer?

But if I stayed, I stood the very real risk of my parents firing me out of spite. The DC area wasn't one you could live in for long without a job.

You don't need a job immediately, the annoying voice of logic in the back of my mind said. *Thanks to Uncle Stan, you have enough money to live off of for a little while at least.*

"Nicole?"

I jerked and dropped my purse. I must have stared blankly into space during the final hymn, because all around me, people flowed out of the church, heading for their cars. The funeral would continue on to the gravesite and then come back to the church for a luncheon prepared by the church's bereavement committee.

Chief Wilson and a woman stood at the end of my pew. The woman had big brown eyes ringed with dark lashes, but the rest of her face was drawn, and a tinge of blue colored her lips. She reminded me of the way a lot of Uncle Stan's heart patients looked, especially in the latter stages.

Chief Wilson tilted his head toward the woman. "This is my wife, Fay. She's not feeling well enough to stay for the rest, but she wanted me to introduce you before we left."

I snagged my purse and scrambled to the end of the pew. "Of course."

Fay grabbed my hand before I had the chance to offer it and held on with a surprisingly tight grip. "I'm not one for public speaking." She cast a look back in the direction of the podium. "But I wanted to add to what so many others have said about what a generous man your uncle was."

Her grip on my hand tightened, and the emerald ring Uncle Stan gave me on my last birthday twisted on my finger. The setting jammed into the skin of the neighboring finger, sending a little dart of pain, and I cringed.

Fay must have misinterpreted my reaction because she patted our clasped hands with her other one. "I know it hurts. We're all going to mourn him. My doctor hasn't been able to figure out what's wrong with my heart. Your uncle had devoted a lot of time in the last couple of weeks to researching my case. He gave me hope for a little while."

A pang that outweighed the pain in my hand shot through my heart. If she'd pinned her last hopes on Uncle Stan, then his death would be an even bigger blow to her than if she'd lost a friend. "I'm very sorry he wasn't able to figure out the cause before—"

She squeezed my hand again and I flinched.

She let me go. "I won't make you talk any more right now. But in the next few days, if you need a shoulder, please call me. I'd like to be able to feel like I've done something for Stan, and I know he'd be happy to know you weren't going through this alone."

He probably would have. And he probably would have been angrier at my parents than I was for leaving me to come up here by myself. It would feel good to spend an hour or two sharing my memories of Uncle Stan with someone before I left. Once I got home, my parents would likely act as if nothing had changed. My only chance to grieve Uncle Stan would be here in Fair Haven.

"Thank you." I gave her a smile that came from my heart. "I might take you up on that."

She fished a piece of paper and a pen out of her purse and wrote down her phone number and address. "Any time. I'm not able to work anymore, so I'd enjoy the company too."

Mark waved to me from the door, and I said my goodbyes to the Wilsons and joined him. He'd picked me up for the funeral. Without his wife. I thought it would be presumptuous to ask why she hadn't come, so all I had was speculation about whether she'd had to work, had hated Uncle Stan, was an invalid, or was locked in their house by Mark who was actually a serial killer after all. I didn't actually believe that last one, but it seemed strange for his wife to not attend, especially when he planned to escort another woman through the day.

A spatter of freezing rain kept the graveside part of the service short, and the luncheon flew by. I only managed to eat about two bites of pasta salad and half of a ham sandwich because a constant stream of Fair Haven residents came to the table, wanting to express their condolences.

I don't know how I managed to make it through without turning into a blubbering mess except that I'd exhausted my supply of tears the night before, after the visitation.

The stream of people was starting to slow down when Mark's cell phone rang. He glanced at the number, walked away from the table, and answered. Part way through the conversation he looked back at me. I gave him a smile and he mouthed the word *work*.

My stomach tensed. Not only was he my ride home, but I didn't want to stay here alone. Mark was the closest thing I had to a friend in this town. If he had to go, would it be rude for me to leave, too?

Mark tucked the phone back into the pocket of his suit and returned to the table.

"You have to go?" I asked.

He nodded. "Let me see if I can find you another ride."

Chief Wilson had already left, and Grant couldn't leave. He was technically in charge even though the luncheon was held in the church. That meant any ride

Mark found me would be with a stranger. That was only slightly more appealing than walking back to my B&B in the freezing rain in my dress and not-warm-enough-for-Michigan coat.

He must have read my hesitance on my face because he quickly squeezed my upper arm. "Don't worry. I have someone in mind."

And for a reason outside the realm of common sense, his assurance did make me less concerned. It probably shouldn't have. I'd been burned before by men who insisted I could trust them and turned out to be liars.

He was back less than five minutes later with a man in his fifties who looked like he'd swallowed a barrel. If someone tipped him over, I wasn't sure he'd be able to get back on his feet again without help.

But he had the warmest smile I'd ever seen.

"This is Russell Dantry," Mark said. "He's the manager of Sugarwood."

"So you're Nikki." Russell shook his head. "I didn't expect you to be so grown up. I knew you had to be since Stan said you were a lawyer now, but so many of his stories featured you as a little girl."

It was an eerie feeling to have someone know so much about you when you knew nothing about them.

He gave my hand a good squeeze, much as Fay had done, and I made a mental note to never wear my emerald ring to a funeral again.

"Stan was my best friend," he said. "Giving you a ride home is the least I can do."

My body was starting to feel like I'd lashed bricks to my wrists and ankles. "Would it be terribly rude to ask for that ride right away?"

"Not at all. It'll be hours yet before everyone else clears out of here, and no one expects you to stay the whole time. I'll pull my truck up front so you don't have to go all the way through the parking lot in the rain."

Another truck. At least I was getting a bit better at maneuvering my way in while wearing a skirt and heels.

I swallowed back a yawn. "Thanks."

Mark gave my shoulder another squeeze and leaned in. "Do you prefer Nikki?"

His warm breath brushed my ear and sent an entirely inappropriate shiver down my arms. I did prefer Nikki, but only Uncle Stan had ever been brave enough to call me that. My parents insisted that they hadn't named me Nikki. They'd named me Nicole. "Perhaps."

"That's what I'll call you then."

And then he was gone, leaving a warm spot on my shoulder and a bit of a bruise on my heart. Why was it that I only attracted married men?

Five minutes later, I nestled into Russ' truck, with the heater blasting. Based on the way his face resembled a steamed beet, I had to guess he'd turned the temperature up ten degrees higher than he liked it for my sake.

"How long do you plan to stay in Fair Haven?" Russ asked as he turned onto the street in front of the church.

"I only have three days left before I'm due back to work." I snuggled down into my coat. The warmth seeped into my bones. At last. "Hopefully that gives me enough time to sort through Uncle Stan's house."

"He left the place to you then?"

There was a strange note in Russ' voice that I couldn't quite identify. Maybe the warmth was making me drowsy, or maybe he was better at hiding his emotions than most people were.

"He did." I trained my gaze onto the rain streaming in diagonal bands along the window instead of looking over at him, a trick I used to make people feel more comfortable. Reading people was an art form, my mom said. A lawyer needed to know when to make eye contact and when to break it to get the most out of someone. "I'll need help understanding how Sugarwood works and making decisions about its future. If you're willing."

I peeked back in his direction.

"'Course, boss." He said it with a grin, and whatever I thought I'd heard in his voice before was gone. "I've been working there since straight out of high school, before Stan ever bought the place. There's not much I can't tell you about it."

Maybe it'd been concern for Sugarwood's future and his job that I'd picked up on before. If he'd never worked anyplace else, a sudden change in ownership must be terrifying. How many sugar bushes could there be in the area to manage if I'd turned out to be a jerk?

The gentle whap-whap of the windshield wipers filled the cab.

I squirmed a little. Some part of my nature had never been comfortable with extended silences. Not sure what that said about me, but it probably wasn't good. "So Uncle Stan talked about me a lot?"

"Nothing embarrassing or private. But he was so proud of you. I almost felt like you were my niece, I knew you so well." His voice hitched a little. "I'm going to miss him."

If he started to cry, there was no way I was going to hold it together. Seeing a man cry was my kryptonite. I needed to change the subject. Fast. To anything else.

My stupid brain stalled out on me and I grabbed the first thing I could form a solid thought around. "How would you feel about me staying on to help run Sugarwood? At least for a little while."

The words came out in a jumble, my voice fast and panicked. But the question felt right somehow.

Uncle Stan wouldn't have left me his business if he hadn't thought I was making the right move to take a little time away from practicing law. He hadn't been willing to make my decision for me, he'd said in his last email, but he wanted me to be careful that I didn't look back on my life some day and regret how I'd spent it. This might be my only chance to figure out what I wanted from my life before the pressure to succeed and live up to what everyone else thought I should do trapped me on a path I didn't necessarily want to be on.

I was so caught up in my thoughts that it took me a minute to realize Russ had answered me and was shooting glances in my direction.

I bit my bottom lip. "Sorry. I think I phased out there for a minute."

"I said I'd much rather have someone here working with me than to run the place alone. But you don't need to feel obligated to stay just 'cause Stan left you the place. He wouldn't have wanted that."

"That's not it. It's..."

I did feel obligated to stay, but not because I owned a business here. If I left without making sure Uncle Stan's death was properly investigated, the guilt would eat me alive. It'd be like I'd abandoned the man who'd always been there when I needed him.

Right now I couldn't seem to sort my emotions about leaving law from my emotions about losing Uncle Stan. I knew myself well enough to know that I wouldn't be able to make a clear-headed decision about Sugarwood and my future until Uncle Stan's murder was solved. Based on Chief Wilson's declaration earlier this week, the only way to ensure that happened was to stay and investigate myself.

I shifted in my seat so I could face Russ better. This time I needed to see his face. I would stay and investigate Uncle Stan's murder one way or another, but I wouldn't move into his house at Sugarwood and learn the business if Russ was against it. This was his life and his world. It might only be a short stop on my journey. It wasn't right to throw his life into chaos in the hope of making mine better.

A wave of nerves hit me out of nowhere, and I sucked my hands back into my sleeves to hide the twitch in my thumb. "I think this is the place I need to be right now. If you don't mind taking on a green-horn."

Russ actually guffawed. "I think you have to be on a ranch to be a greenhorn."

"And that shows how much I know about farm life right there. So would you be alright with me staying and learning the business? It might not be permanent."

"I'll teach you whatever you want to know. Sugar-wood means a lot to me"—that strange note was back in his voice again—"and I'd like to know that the person who owns her cares about her too."

"Thanks. I appreciate it."

He nodded and I faced the window again. I could barely make out the outline of The Sunburnt Arms ahead through the rain.

Now all I had to do was figure out how to investigate a case with "no leads," as Chief Wilson had so bluntly pointed out. That, and tell my parents I planned to stay in Fair Haven indefinitely.

Chapter 7

I put off the phone call to my parents. The longer I waited, the worse it would be, but my courage failed me. Calling them not only meant facing their wrath. It also meant committing to staying here. It meant traveling back to Virginia for my belongings and sub-leasing my apartment.

It felt huge and overwhelming.

Focusing on catching a killer, ironically enough, felt easier even though my one experience in the past with investigating had been a disaster and had been what finally pushed me to ask Uncle Stan's advice about changing careers and risking excommunication by my parents.

By the time Russ picked me up the next morning for my tour of Sugarwood's grounds, I'd decided that the best place to start digging into who might have killed Uncle Stan was to simply ask Russ. He'd been Uncle Stan's best friend. If anyone would know about a grudge someone held against my uncle, it would be him.

He pulled his truck into a gravel parking lot. I hadn't seen it through the trees when I came to the house with Chief Wilson and Mark. The lot butted up to two buildings that sat about the width of a football field apart.

Russ pointed to the smaller of the two. "That's the pump house. The sap from the trees comes down a system of tubes to the pump house, and from there we pump it into those vats."

He nodded in the direction of cylindrical storage tanks that looked big enough to hold his pickup truck. The tanks nestled up to the side of the larger building, with its gray sides and green roof.

"The other building is our sugar shack," he said.

I sank back in my seat. "I think I might have underestimated the scope of Uncle Stan's business."

Russ chuckled. "A lot of people do. We're a commercial operation with over 15,000 trees, but when people hear *sugar shack*, they think about a wooden hut out in the woods. We do still have the original small sugar shack used over a hundred years ago when the first owner started tapping the sugar maples on his property, but we use it for the guided tours now."

His laughter reminded me of how I'd imagined Santa Claus would sound back when I was a little kid. "But this is where the sap turns into maple syrup?"

"And maple butter and maple sugar. We have a separate building for putting together the candy and such, and a pancake house open year-round with a connected store. There's also a stable near the original sugar shack for the horses and sleigh we use to take guests out into the woods in the winter. The snowshoe rentals happen from the office on the side of the stable as well."

I definitely had not had the right picture about what Uncle Stan did with his time. When I'd asked to learn the business, I'd imagined spending my time stirring a vat of sticky goo with plenty of alone time to mull over my life.

Russ pushed open his truck door. "Let me show you."

Inside the building, he walked me through the process, starting with the reverse osmosis machines for separating out some of the water from the sap. Apparently that sped up the process and gave them more control over the final product. They stored the pure water they extracted to use for cleaning the pipelines after the maple syrup season.

We finished with the stainless-steel evaporators—the modern way of boiling the sap until it turned thick and sweet. Each of the evaporators were long enough that I could have lain down inside. At the moment, they were empty and still.

So was the building, except for one man at the far end, tinkering with the insides of one of the evaporators. "Where is everyone? You must need more people than this to run things."

"It's the off-season. We have seasonal workers who help during the busy season, and then our full-time staff maintains things the rest of the year."

All of those people could be potential suspects. Chief Wilson's words about poking at rocks just to see what came out made more sense now.

Problem was, I didn't necessarily want to come right out and ask Russ if any of them would have had a reason to kill Uncle Stan. It wasn't public knowledge yet that his death was no longer considered an accidental overdose or suicide. The more people who knew, the more likely the small-town gossip mill would spread it everywhere. Right now, the killer would feel safe. Once word got out, he or she would be more vigilant.

We left the modern sugar shack, and Russ led the way down a well-manicured trail that he said extended for miles and was used by hikers in the summer. At this time of year, the trees were bare three-quarters of the way up, only their tops still bright red with leaves.

"The employees..." I picked up a maple leaf and spun it around in my fingers. "They all seem content? No major complaints?"

Russ' bushy eyebrows drew down until they almost touched in the middle. "You should know your uncle better than that. He took good care of his employees."

Grrr. I scuffed my toe into the leaves at the side of the trail. I clearly hadn't thought through the implications of that question well enough.

Maybe there wasn't a way to find out what I wanted to know without asking Russ directly. "What I meant was do you know if there was anyone who might want to hurt my uncle? Had he had an argument with anyone lately?"

His face went unnaturally still, as if he was trying not to react. "The police said Stan died because of something he did to himself."

"They found new evidence," I said softly. "Chief Wilson told me they've reopened the investigation."

He turned away and continued down the trail. I scurried after him.

The trail opened up into another clearing. A driveway came into the same spot from the opposite direction.

Russ pointed to the larger of the two buildings. "That's the stable." He patted the front of the smaller building. "And this is the original sugar shack."

Normally I would respect someone's desire not to talk about a personal topic, but this was different. This had become a case. Besides, I was in too deep. He knew the truth about Uncle Stan's death now. I needed to get something out of it in return in case the cost was everyone in town learning about it.

"I'm only trying to find out the truth," I said.

"The truth is, even if someone did argue with Stan, that doesn't mean they'd want to kill him. People fight. It don't mean nothing." He unlocked a padlock on the front of the sugar shack, and slid the door open. "This is probably more what you were imagining."

It was. The "shack" was equipped with old-fashioned maple syrup equipment, including a small wood-fired boiler, all set up for demonstration purposes. Seeing it close-up, I felt stupid for imagining this was how they still made maple syrup. You could make enough in this building for yourself, but not to sell and make a living from.

"This hinged front door isn't original, of course," Russ was saying. "We added that to help with tours and keep the equipment safe at night."

I'd go along with his attempted side track for a minute to give him some space and then circle back around to his comment about *if someone did argue with Stan*. He hadn't denied that someone had.

I stepped up into the building. "You had problems with people damaging the equipment?"

Russ clamped a bungee cord onto the eye in the sliding door. The door bulged back against it as if wanting to close again. "Teenagers mostly. Before we had a solid door we could lock, they'd come in here at night to fool around, drink, smoke. You know the stuff kids do. Sometimes we'd find damage in the morning. Mostly your uncle was worried they'd light a fire in here for warmth and accidentally burn the place down."

"You don't think—"

"No." Russ' voice was sharp. "I don't. They were kids and it was years ago."

He spun around more quickly than someone of his shape should and laid a hand on the bungee cord. "Hey, did your uncle ever tell you the story of how we got ourselves trapped in here the first day we installed this door? We didn't realize when we built it that the house sloped in the opposite direction and the door would always slam closed if it wasn't hooked."

Russ chattered on and I scrubbed my hands along the front of my jeans. How could I rephrase my questions to make them less objectionable to him? Was it that he didn't want to think someone he knew might have harmed Uncle Stan? Or did he know something and he was afraid whoever came after Stan would come after him? I didn't have enough information to even guess.

By the time I focused back on Russ, I'd missed most of his story.

He laughed. "After we'd been missing a good day, Noah reported it to the chief."

"Noah?"

"He's the one who maintains the equipment in the production building. You saw him when we were there."

I nodded absently. Maybe if I came at it from the point of view that it wasn't fair a murderer walked around enjoying their life while we'd had to attend Uncle Stan's funeral. Surely Russ had a sense of justice. "So what happened? Who found you?"

"Carl." He paused. "Chief Wilson, you know. And he nearly falls over laughing at us. We've never lived that down, especially since it was the first time Stan and Carl met. The latch still sticks enough that you can't get out if you accidentally close the door while you're in here. That's why we put on the hook." He tapped his fingers on it. "We always meant to fix the latch so no one else would lock themselves in here by mistake, but something more important kept coming along. And it made for such a great story."

He waved toward the driveway. "Come on. I'll show you the shop and pancake house next."

We stepped down from the building and he closed and padlocked the door.

He must have read my expression when he turned around because he sighed. "You're so much like your uncle. You're not going to let this go, are you?"

I'd heard that before—that I was more like Uncle Stan than like my own parents. "Can you think of anyone I should at least talk to? Anyone at all."

"This isn't the big city you're used to. This is a small town full of people who've known each other their whole lives. No one here would want to kill Stan. Whatever the police think they've found, I don't believe it means someone I've known my whole life is a killer."

That explained my earlier question about why he was so resistant to even talking about it. I didn't like the idea myself. In my nightmares I'd see Uncle Stan begging someone, a friend, a co-worker, not to do this. Still, it was better than the alternative—that he was so depressed that he gave up on what he believed in and couldn't face another day. "You'd rather believe he killed himself?"

Russ looked away.

"Don't you want to know who murdered your best friend? See them go to prison for what they've done?"

"Of course I would. But most of what you're going to dig up by asking questions will only be misunderstandings, and you'll cast suspicion on good people. This is a tourist town. People lose their jobs for less. If Stan was murdered"—he wagged a finger—"*if* he was, let the police look into it. It's not your place."

A heavy weight settled on my chest. Russ had a point. If I wasn't subtle about this, I could leave a black spot on the reputation of someone who had nothing to do with Uncle Stan's death. I didn't want that.

But maybe I could use my outsider status to my advantage. I was Stan's grieving niece. Wouldn't people want to tell me all their stories, the same way Russ had wanted to share the goofy story about locking themselves in the sugar shack? And since I planned to move here, I had good reason to want to know more about the ins and outs of the town.

I couldn't simply walk up to a stranger on the street and start quizzing them, though. I'd have to begin with the people I'd already met. Like Fay. It was time to take her up on that invitation to visit.

Chapter 8

After finishing my tour of Sugarwood, I walked the twenty minutes from The Sunburnt Arms to Fay's house, the jar of maple butter I'd selected from Sugarwood's store as a gift tucked into my purse.

My car still wasn't ready, and Quantum Mechanics was closed on Sunday, so I'd be carless for at least another day. Russ had offered to chauffeur me around, but I had to try to acclimate to the northern weather sooner or later. Instead, we had plans to have supper together tomorrow night.

I'd half expected things between us to be awkward after my attempt to pull information out of him, but the rest of my tour had been like being with an old friend. We'd swapped more stories about Uncle Stan, and I'd learned about making maple syrup candy. If my waistline could handle it, I suspected I'd spend most of my time dealing with the store and pancake house and leave the actual production elements to Russ and the other staff.

I checked the map I'd printed off one more time and turned down Orchard Street. The Wilsons' house nestled at the end of a cul-de-sac with what must have been a beautiful view of the lake from a back balcony if they had one.

I knocked on the door and Fay answered immediately. She didn't look any healthier than when I'd seen her at the funeral. If anything, more of the color was gone from her face.

She ushered me inside. "Carl's at the office again today, so it's lovely to have company. Since he insisted I quit working, it gets quite lonely at times."

She led me into a sunny kitchen decorated in yellows and whites. She'd laid out the table with shortbread cookies and crackers next to a jar of maple syrup butter.

"I thought you'd like to try some of your Uncle Stan's products," Fay said. "Coffee or tea?"

I gave her the jar I'd brought, which we had a good laugh over, and settled in with a cup of coffee that was substantially better than the strong-enough-to-grow-chest-hair-on-a-woman brew served at The Sunburnt Arms. If I had a firstborn child, I might have traded them away for a grande non-fat mocha latte from Starbucks. I didn't know all of Fair Haven, but I'd yet to see a Starbucks anywhere.

Fifteen minutes into our visit, Fay stopped mid-sentence and pressed a hand to her chest.

I jumped to my feet, but she waved me away.

"It'll pass." She leaned back in her chair and drew in a long breath. "That time it felt like butterflies were in my heart trying to break out."

I eased back into my chair, but stayed on the edge. "And the doctors don't know what's wrong?"

Fay pushed her plate away from her, as if she'd lost interest in what was on it. "My doctor has no idea. Stan was looking through all my files and was trying to help solve the mystery. But then..." She shrugged. "I have more than one reason to miss him."

Her doctor belonged on my list of suspects—a list of one so far. Maybe he'd made a mistake and didn't want Stan to find out about it. A misdiagnosis could hurt a doctor's career, couldn't it? "Your doctor didn't mind someone else stepping in?"

"Not that I know of. Once I told him who I wanted to bring in to consult, he called your uncle himself. He copied all my medical records and sent them to Stan without even charging me for it."

That didn't sound much like a man who had something big enough to hide that he'd kill over it. It sounded more like a doctor who truly cared about his patients.

More color had drained from Fay's face, and dark circles ringed her eyes.

Tension spiraled through my shoulders. "Should I call someone for you?"

Fay shook her head. "But I think I might need to cut our visit short and ask if you'd help me to the couch."

I packed away the treats where Fay told me and washed out our cups. We only touched on the topic I'd really wanted to talk to her about today, but I wasn't about to put her health at risk. Uncle Stan was gone. A few more days one way or another wouldn't matter to him now.

Fay had two inches or more in height on me, so I ducked under her arm and supported her to the couch. I jogged back to the kitchen and poured her a glass of water. I left it and her cell phone within easy reach.

Fay grabbed my hand. "Thank you for coming today. People around here...they mean well, but I think they only see my illness anymore. It was nice to be talked to like a person for a while rather than like a sick person."

"It was my pleasure."

And it was. The longer I spent in Fair Haven, the more I got to know the people, the more I liked it here. I could see why Uncle Stan loved this place.

It made it all the more disturbing that one of them had killed him.

I slung my purse over my shoulder. Before I left, I wanted to clear up one quick thing that had been niggling at me. "How did you know Uncle Stan used to be a cardiologist? It doesn't seem like he told many people here about it." Not even Mark, who was a doctor himself.

Red blotches bloomed in the middle of Fay's pale cheeks, giving her the appearance of a clown in faded make-up. "I was out walking, on one of the trails at Sugarwood. I overheard Stan arguing with someone. I pieced together that it was the son of a former patient of his. I was curious, so I searched for his name on the computer when I got home."

No one reached the heights in their medical career that Uncle Stan had without losing a few patients along the way. Especially since he'd built his reputation on taking high-risk and unusual cases.

The weight that had been crushing my shoulders eased. Maybe someone here hadn't killed him. Maybe an angry family member of a former patient had tracked him down. I liked that theory much better. "How long ago was this?"

Fay shrugged. "A couple of weeks at most." She rubbed at the spot above her heart again. "I truly am sorry we had to end our visit so soon. How about we plan for a raincheck? Once your car is running again, I could show you around town." She rolled her eyes. "I'd drive myself, but my doctor pulled my license."

I smiled at her, but it hurt something inside. There was a reason, beyond my parents and my tendency to faint at the sight of blood, that I'd chosen a legal career over a medical one. I couldn't stand the thought of losing people. A doctor invested so much time into finding ways to keep their patients healthy. How did every death not feel like a soul-crushing failure?

Instead of saying any of that, I said, "It's a date."

I turned to go, but Fay took my hand again. "You don't think the man I heard arguing with Stan killed him do you?" She pursed her lips. "Carl told me about the investigation being reopened."

Since she already knew and she was the wife of the chief, I couldn't think of any reason not to be honest with her. "I don't know, but I'm going to dig around and hopefully find out."

Fay tightened her hold. It seemed like a pattern with her, like it was how she sought connection. Thankfully this time I'd left my emerald ring behind.

"Be careful," she said. "And let me know what you find out, will you?"

I nodded and slipped out the door. Russ' poor reaction to my questions had left me without a confidante on my quest. As much as I wanted to share what I was doing with Mark—we'd started out on this quest together—he was a married man, and experience had taught me the dangers lurking there.

Any married man who flirted with a woman who wasn't his wife couldn't be trusted. And I already had a town full of people I couldn't trust.

Chapter 9

After turning off of Fay's street, I hurried back to my B&B. As I'd discovered during my attempt to book a room before driving up here, Fair Haven had only one place for travelers to stay during the off-season—The Sunburnt Arms. Since Uncle Stan's angry visitor had been here not that long ago, they must have stayed at the same place I was.

Fay's information couldn't have come at a better time. Since Uncle Stan's house was mine now, I had to get over my twitchiness about it being the spot where he died. Chief Wilson's crime scene investigators had finished their second sweep of Uncle Stan's house, and they'd released it for me to move in to, which I planned to do tomorrow. If I'd already left the B&B, it'd look suspicious for me to go back and poke around.

I jogged up the front steps of The Sunburnt Arms and slowed to a casual walk as I entered. Instead of heading for my room, I settled in to one of the cushy armchairs in the lobby and acted like I was checking messages on my phone.

Other than the amenities needed to attract guests, The Sunburnt Arms had tried to keep as much old-world charm as possible. The room key I'd been given was an actual key, not a key card. And even though they had a credit card machine for processing payments and a computer to track everything, they also had an old-fashioned guest book laid out on the check-in counter. When I'd first arrived, the desk clerk insisted I sign it.

So if I could get my hands on the guest book, I'd have some leads to follow up on as to who Uncle Stan's unhappy visitor was—assuming he'd stayed overnight. I doubted anyone would drive roundtrip from Northern Virginia to Michigan and back without an overnight stay, but I suppose it was theoretically possible if one wanted to drink a lot of caffeine.

So how could I get possession of the guest book?

I glanced up from my phone. The guy behind the desk this afternoon wasn't one of the regular weekday staff I'd chatted with before. It wasn't like he was going to hand it over to me and let me take pictures of all the pages. That had to violate some privacy law or something, assuming the laws here were anything like the ones in Virginia. I might have had a chance anyway if the clerk on duty was Mandy. Mandy was in her sixties and seemed to have a new mystery novel in her hands every time I walked by. I might have been able to convince her to help me in my amateur sleuthing. But whoever he was, he certainly was no Mandy.

This guy was somewhere in his mid-twenties, with acne scars and too much gel in his hair. If I had any game, I might have tried flirting with him to sneak a peek at the book, but my attempts at flirting looked a little too much like an ostrich trying to learn to dance. I'd been told by friends back home that it was actually painful to watch.

That left me with the option of luring him away from the desk.

I left the lobby and went down the hallway until I reached the staircase. I needed to find a space to wait where I could see him go by, but I also needed to be close enough to run back to the desk before he returned.

There weren't any guest rooms on the first floor, only the lobby out front and the dining room, kitchen, and laundry at the back. If I camped out in any of the rooms at the back, I wouldn't know for sure when he passed, and I couldn't call him for help from the lobby.

I turned in a slow circle. The hall didn't even have a large potted plant to hide behind. It did have what was probably a janitor's closet built in under the stairs.

I tried the door handle. It wasn't locked.

There also wasn't very much room. I wiggled in around a stack of buckets and straddled a vacuum. I eased the door shut.

My eyes adjusted slowly to the dark, giving me plenty of time to hear my mother's voice in my head. *This isn't what we do, Nicole. Lawyers don't hide in closets.*

I told her to shut it—something I'd never dare to do in real life—and dialed the front desk.

"Sunburnt Arms. This is Tim. How can I help you today?"

I'd been so focused on finding a place to hide that I hadn't planned out how, exactly, to convince him to leave the front desk.

"Uhhh, yes, this is Room 5. I think my...bathroom tap might be broken."

I shifted around and something sharp poked me in the butt cheek. I yelped.

"Are you alright?" Tim's voice asked.

Crap. "Yeah, I just turned the water on too hot."

"I thought the tap was broken."

I was apparently as bad a liar as I was a flirt. "It is. I mean the cold water isn't working. When I turn it on, I get hot water."

"Right." His voice had that careful tone people tended to use with someone who was talking crazy. "I'll call a plumber, and we'll get it fixed for you as soon as possible."

"No." It was more a screech than anything. This was not going well. Next time I planned to lie, I was going to come up with something really good ahead of time and think through all the possible ways it could go wrong. "I was hoping you could just come up and check it for me...In case, I'm doing it wrong."

I face-palmed. By tomorrow the whole town would have heard the story about Stan's stupid niece who didn't know how to turn on a tap. Perfect, Nikki. Just perfect.

"Okaaay." He stretched the word out, giving it extra syllables, like he was thinking over whether or not I was crazy enough to be a threat to his safety. "Room 5, you said."

"Yes. Room 5."

"I'll be right up."

I slumped against the vacuum. It tipped forward and I slammed my forehead into a mop handle. I bit my cheek to keep from crying out and giving myself away.

Note to self: Clumsy people should never hide in broom closets. It had the same odds of turning out badly as handing a child a pair of scissors and asking them to run an obstacle course.

Clumping footsteps passed overhead. It had to be Tim heading up to my room.

I wouldn't have long. He might only knock once or twice before giving up when I didn't answer.

I burst out of the broom closet, half tripping over the bucket, skidded down the hallway, and stopped just shy of ramming into the front desk. I spun the guest book around and flipped the page over.

I hadn't been paying attention when I signed in. This book was new. My signature was on the back of the first page. The dates on the front of the page were all too recent.

Where would they keep the older guest books? Would they keep them? I had to think that a place like this would hang on to the old books as a badge of honor or something like that. What other reason could there be for making people sign them?

I pivoted around. The books weren't on the shelves behind me.

Tim would be back any second now. My heart pounded in my chest so hard it felt like it was going to burst out like the creature in *Alien*. Not that I'd ever seen that movie—I didn't like anything that kept me awake at night—but I'd heard about it.

Focus, Nicole. I gave myself a mental shake. *You're panicking.*

I opened the cupboard below the check-in desk. Jackpot. I pulled out the top book and quickly checked the dates. It was the one I needed, but I was out of time to take pictures on my phone of the right pages.

I'd have to take it with me. No one would know it was missing, and I could—somehow—return it later.

I straightened up and came face to face with Mark across the desk.

I gasped and dropped the guest book. It hit the floor with a bang.

"What are you doing?" Mark asked at the same time as Tim's voice came from the hallway saying, "What's going on out there?"

I snatched the book back up, skittered around the desk, and grabbed Mark's hand, dragging him outside and down the porch steps. I pulled him around the corner and behind the juniper bushes.

The space between the building and the junipers was tighter than I'd expected. My back and one leg ended up wedged against Mark. Warmth flooded my body and my stomach pitched sideways. Somehow I was still holding his hand. I dropped it.

The front door creaked open and Tim's distinctive clumpy steps crossed the wooden porch.

Mark shifted behind me. "What the h—"

I twisted my arm backward and jammed my fingers across his lips. My mind might have been playing tricks on me, but I'd swear I felt him smile.

The heat in my stomach moved up into my face. This was going to be incredibly awkward to explain afterward.

With Mark's chest pressed against my back, I could feel every breath he took. Tim couldn't have taken more than ten or fifteen seconds before he went back inside, but it felt like a whole lot longer.

Finally the front door creaked again, and I exhaled the breath I'd been holding. I wormed my way out from behind the bush.

Mark picked a piece of juniper out of his collar. His mouth quirked a little, but I didn't know him well enough to figure out whether he was amused or ready to haul me back inside to account for my crimes. "Want to tell me what that was about now?"

I instinctively clasped the guest book to my chest. "It's a long story."

He made a go-on gesture with his hand.

For the first time it hit me that what I'd done could be considered theft, even though when I'd taken the book I'd thought of it as borrowing. That didn't make it much better, since joyriding was still a crime. All the heat drained from my body, and the words shot out of me. "I borrowed...stole a guest book. I'm not going to keep it. I just needed to look at the guests in it to figure out who visited Uncle Stan this month—"

Mark loosened my grip on the book and took my hand in his. "Slow down. Take a deep breath and start again."

I did what he told me, though it was almost impossible to slow my heart rate down when he was holding my hand, and started over, this time from what Chief Wilson said about not having the manpower to chase after a case that would almost undoubtedly go cold. All the way up to nabbing the book.

And by then I was calm enough to act like a grown-up again. I freed my hand and straightened my shoulders. "Are you going to turn me in?"

"No." Now he definitely looked half annoyed, half amused. "But we need to return this guest book today."

We? Part of me liked the sound of that, and part of me—the smarter part—was flashing sirens and warning lights at the other part. I shouldn't accept his help. "I'm okay to handle this on my own."

He jutted his chin toward the book that I still cradled close. "How many names do you think are in there?"

Alright, he had a point there. I could use help going through the book and checking which men were the most likely suspects. And wouldn't it make it more legitimate if the county medical examiner helped me sort through the names? "You're sure you want to become my accomplice in crime?"

He snorted. "You haven't left me much of a choice. Come on."

He headed around the back of The Sunburnt Arms and into the parking lot. He opened the passenger side door of his truck for me.

I hung back. "Where are we going?"

"My house." He gestured toward The Sunburnt Arms. "Unless you want to try to sneak that guest book past the clerk and up into your room."

Actually, I didn't want to do either of those things. And I most definitely did *not* want Mark in my room.

I gnawed on my bottom lip. No sane man would take another woman to the house he shared with his wife, would he? Not unless his intentions were "honorable," as my grandma used to say. Maybe Mark had one of those personalities whose friendliness came across as more intimate and personal than he intended. If he planned to go back to his house to sort through the names in the guest book, he didn't have a problem with his wife seeing me. I might even finally get to meet her. It would be nice to continue building friendships here.

And it wouldn't be the first time I'd projected my attraction onto a man who wasn't interested in me romantically. Lucky in love I was not.

He quirked an eyebrow at me. "Are you coming?"

I climbed up into his truck, grateful I'd worn jeans again today. Soon I'd either need to find a laundromat or make the trip home for more clothes. I'd only brought enough to last me through Tuesday, plus an emergency set.

He backed his truck out of the parking spot and turned onto the road. "I've known Carl for as long as I've been the medical examiner here. Even short-handed, he'll do the best he can to solve this."

He probably would. For all his crustiness, he didn't seem like a bad guy. And based on what I'd gathered from Fay, he did spend more time than any man should at his job. Still... "I can't take that risk. I owe it to my uncle to at least try to help catch whoever killed him."

He glanced at me sideways. "Will you promise me that you won't go rogue and steal anything else?"

I chuckled. "I promise. I scared myself enough this time. Can you imagine the headlines? *Top Defense Attorneys' Daughter Arrested for Petty Theft.* My parents would disown me."

He pulled into the driveway of a cottage that looked like someone copied it from a Thomas Kincade painting, all gray stone walls and blue doors and shutters. A dormant lilac tree grew on each side of the front door. The smell in the springtime must be intoxicating.

The house was nothing like what I'd expected from the county medical examiner. Most successful doctors in the DC area lived in palatial homes in the best neighborhoods. Of course, Mark was technically a civil servant, so maybe that made a difference. Or maybe he and his wife preferred a simpler lifestyle.

Whatever the reason, the house was so adorable that I wanted to hug it.

"Have you told them yet that you're staying?"

I hopped out of the truck. "What?"

"Your parents."

"Oh. No." I hurried ahead of him so that he wouldn't press more. I didn't want to talk about my parents right now. "How'd you find out?"

He unlocked the door and gave me that crooked smile that showed off his dimples. "Small town. Nothing stays secret for very long around here."

"I'll remember that."

Inside the house, I kicked off my shoes in the spot where he pointed and instantly wanted to put them back on. I'd forgotten which socks I'd chosen to wear today. The socks themselves were gray, but they were covered in tiny black monkeys wearing purple bow ties.

I'd always chafed at the "boring" clothes my mom forced me to wear when I was a child and at the professional attire I had to wear once I entered law school. My quirky socks were my silent rebellion against it. No one ever saw my socks, so it hadn't seemed like a problem. When I got dressed today, I hadn't counted on what must be a Northern custom of taking off your shoes indoors, and I hadn't minded Fay seeing my monkey socks earlier.

For a second I thought I caught Mark smirking. He turned away and headed over to the couch in the adjoining living room. I trailed after him, but not before noticing that there weren't any ladies' shoes in the entrance way other than mine. Was he married but separated?

The pictures lining the fireplace mantel told a different story. A younger Mark, without gray in his hair, in a tux, kissing a slender blonde in a wedding gown. Mark and the same blonde on horseback, somewhere near mountains.

Mark and a pregnant blonde in a park with a dog that looked at least half lab. His hand was on her belly and the proud grin on his face punctured my heart.

He wasn't just married. He was a father. So where were they?

I lifted the photo with the dog as casually as I could. "Your wife?"

"Yeah."

Was that a flinch?

He stepped backward. "I've got a laptop and a tablet in the other room that we can use to run searches on these names. I'll grab them and be right back. If you want anything to drink, help yourself."

Whatever the situation, he clearly didn't want to talk about it. I grabbed two sodas from the fridge and settled onto the couch.

When Mark came back, he quickly focused the conversation onto how to divide up the names. Two hours and a delivered pizza later, he held up his tablet.

"I found one that lives in Virginia," he said, "assuming it's the same guy. I think it must be. I can't imagine too many men are named Edgar Poe."

"Not unless their parents wanted them to be taunted as a child."

"Or unless it was an alias."

I hadn't considered that the man might have left a false name in the guest book. Fingers crossed that wasn't the case. I pulled out my cell phone. "What's the number?"

Mark read it off and I dialed. Then he moved in close so that his ear was almost next to mine. My breath caught.

"Edgar Poe," a voice on the other end of the line said.

"Are you—" My voice cracked and I steadied it. "Are you the Mr. Edgar Poe who recently visited Stan Dawes?"

"I am. Who is this?"

He'd admitted it so easily that my instincts said he'd had nothing to do with Uncle Stan's death. Either that or he was a practiced liar who knew the best lies were doppelgangers of the truth.

I'd already thought up what tactic I was going to use this time, but I was going to stick as closely to the truth as possible as well. I'd learned my lesson from making up crazy stories on the fly.

"I'm Nicole Fitzhenry." My dad would be mortified that I'd dropped the Dawes even temporarily, but I thought it was best if Edgar didn't realize right away that Stan was my uncle. "I'm taking care of a few things for Dr. Dawes, and your name and phone number were on his to-do list. I'm just following up."

"That's really good of him." Edgar's voice sounded happy. Not at all the way I'd expect someone with a guilty conscience to sound. "My dad's actually supposed to be able to come home next week, and Dr. Khaw is optimistic about his chances. Could you tell Dr. Dawes how much my family appreciated the favor he called in for us? I'm sure Dad would be dead now if it wasn't for his help. And..."

I let the silence stretch.

"And..." Edgar cleared his throat. "Could you tell him I'm sorry for blowing up at him the way I did? It wasn't right of me. He's retired and he didn't owe my dad anything even though he was his doctor the first time his heart gave out. Do you think I should send a card or something?"

"That's okay," I said softly. "I'll make sure he knows."

"Thanks." Edgar's exhale came clearly through the phone. "I appreciate it."

We disconnected the call.

Mark leaned back on the couch.

I flopped back beside him. "I don't think he's our guy."

"Nope," Mark said. "Sounds like whatever beef he had with Stan got resolved pretty quick."

Which meant I was back to where I started, without any suspects. Tomorrow I'd continue searching through Uncle Stan's papers and other files and see if anything turned up.

"Would you like a glass of wine?" Mark asked. "Or a cup of coffee?"

I stifled a yawn and clamped the guest book closed with a thump. I glanced at my watch. It wasn't exactly late, but I was emotionally drained. "Thanks, but I ought to get this thing back."

Mark went for his keys, and we were back in the parking lot of The Sunburnt Arms within a few minutes.

"Thanks again for your help today." I pushed open the truck door. "I forgot to ask. Why were you at The Sunburnt Arms this afternoon anyway?"

Mark scrubbed a hand over the fresh stubble on his face. He looked as drained as I felt. "Since I heard you were planning to stay, I was going to offer you a tour of Fair Haven. But then today turned out a little differently then I'd planned." He grinned. "Maybe tomorrow we could grab a non-pizza dinner and I'll show you around?"

I missed the truck's running board, hit the ground hard, and stumbled forward. I was no Bachelorette, but that sounded an awful lot like a date.

Chapter 10

Monday morning I was sitting in Uncle Stan's living room, surrounded by my mountainous *Keep* and *Trash* piles and the boxes of papers I still needed to sort through, when my cell phone rang. The caller ID flashed *Mom*.

Since my original departure date was supposed to be tomorrow morning, I really needed to answer and break the news to her. But the timing was terrible. When I closed my eyes, I could still see the confusion on Mark's face as I turned down his invitation. I didn't need to disappoint another person so soon.

Telling Mark that I'd already agreed to let Fay show me around and that I'd planned to have dinner with Russ tonight had softened it some, but it was only a matter of time. I didn't need any more complication in my life, and his martial situation—whatever it was—screamed complication in five languages. He was still wearing his wedding ring, for Pete's sake. What did he expect? If he and his wife were separated and he still loved her enough to keep wearing his ring, I wasn't about to become the rebound or time-killer that filled the gap until they got back together.

The phone rang the final time before it would switch to voice mail.

I swiped my finger across the answer key. "Hi Mom."

"Could you come into the office as soon as you get in tomorrow instead of waiting until Wednesday morning?"

No *How was the funeral?* No *How are you handling it all?* Just a *How soon can you get back to work?*

"What's going on?" I asked, dodging her question for the moment.

She let out a dramatic sigh. "Evelyn's doctor put her on bed rest until the baby's born. We haven't had time yet to even interview for a replacement, and now we're short-handed two months ahead of schedule."

Few things in life were more annoying to my mother than someone disrupting her schedule.

This did not bode well for my news. I had to think of this like tearing off a Band-Aid. It was going to hurt either way. I might as well make it quick. "I'm not going to be back tomorrow night as planned."

Dead silence. I glanced at the phone to make sure the call hadn't dropped. "Mom?"

"What do you mean you won't be back tomorrow? When will you be back?"

"I won't be coming back permanently. Uncle Stan left me his business here."

"Nicole Elizabeth."

Oh, crap. She'd pulled out the middle name.

"This is not what we do." I could imagine the look on her face. The one that made even judges tremble. "Your uncle had an illness and it affected his judgment, but you can't possibly be considering giving up the potential of a successful legal career to chase chickens, or whatever it is he raised there, around a farmyard."

I bet her lip curled on that last word.

The sign I'd seen multiple times while driving up here popped into my head. "Farmers feed cities, Mom."

The silence again.

Arg. Giving her lip wasn't going to make this better. "It's not that kind of farm anyway. He made maple syrup."

"Is that supposed to make me feel better about my daughter throwing away her career, her life?"

The teenage comeback of *It's my life* floated to the tip of my tongue. I swallowed it down. It formed into a lump in my stomach. Was this simply some delayed rebellious phase that I'd regret later?

"I'm not giving up on being a lawyer." At least not yet. "Think of this more like a sabbatical while I figure out what I want to do with my life."

"What you want to do with your life." She said it in the same tone of voice as someone else might say *Join a cult* or *Become a nudist.* "I told your father we shouldn't have let you go alone."

I recoiled from the phone. She made it sound like I was still an impressionable child who couldn't make good decisions and needed to be monitored all the time. "I'll let you know when I'll be back to pick up my things."

"Nicole, wait." Her voice softened. "It's halfway across the country away from us and from your friends. Are you sure about this?"

No. "Yes, I'm sure."

"Call me regularly to let me know you're alright. I'll miss you."

An unexpected lump formed in my throat. I always knew my parents loved me, but my mom had never been the nurturing type. When I'd scrape my knee as a kid, instead of cuddling away my tears, she'd ask *Now what can we learn from this?* "I'll miss you too."

"And don't expect me to like what you're doing or to stop trying to convince you to come back here where you belong."

Now that sounded more like my mom. "Understood."

"I've got to go. Apparently, I have to hire *two* temporary replacements."

She disconnected the call before I could say anything else. At least that was one unpleasant task over with. Soon the dirty laundry Uncle Stan left behind would be done in the washing machine as well.

That's something no one ever seems to talk about. What do you do about the deceased person's dirty laundry and toiletries? Where did you dispose of their medications? What about the private knickknacks and other items that meant something to them but nothing to you? It felt wrong to toss it all into the trash or give it away.

I blew out a puff of air, pulled the next banker's box toward me, and flipped off the lid. The words on the side read BUSINESS PAPERS in Uncle Stan's clear, boxy print. His handwriting had always been too neat for a doctor's.

The folders inside the box held employee contracts and ownership papers. I assumed all the rest of the receipts and records would be kept in Russ' office, wherever that was, since he was the manager.

I opened the last folder to make sure I wasn't missing anything that would need my prompt attention or would lead to a clue. It wasn't labeled, but that didn't mean that what was inside didn't matter. After yesterday's phone call crossed my only suspect off the list, I'd decided that I wouldn't assume anything about Uncle Stan's papers. I'd examine each one closely just in case.

It was either that or admit that Chief Wilson was right and Uncle Stan's case was a dead end.

I scanned the papers. It was a business partnership agreement between Uncle Stan and Russ, but the papers weren't signed. Neither Russ nor Tom McClanahan had said anything about it.

This must be why Russ acted so strangely when he learned that I'd inherited the business from Uncle Stan. If they'd been in the middle of negotiating a partnership, he'd probably hoped Uncle Stan would have left him the business in his will.

Guilt fluttered in my stomach. I needed to talk to Russ. It wasn't fair that I swooped in, knowing nothing about the business, and took it over. Maybe we could still come to some agreement, assuming he'd want to partner with me.

I scooped up the papers along with my purse and phone and left the house. Russ mentioned yesterday that he lived on the grounds, pointing at a trail that led off behind the store. It was almost time for our dinner anyway, and it wouldn't take me too long to walk there. By now I was used to walking everywhere, though thankfully I should have my car back by tomorrow.

The sun hung low in the sky, stretching emaciated fingers of light over the trees and making it seem like the shadows were reaching out to snatch at me. Shiver spiders crawled across my skin.

I broke into a jog. Why were there no streetlights out here? How did they expect people to function after sunset without streetlights? Who knew what kind of creatures lived in the woods?

I turned the corner, spotted Russ's house, and sprinted for it. I banged on the door.

It opened and Russ stood in the doorway, backlit. "Nikki? What's wrong?"

"Nothing." My gasping breaths put the lie into my words. "I guess I got a little freaked out by how little light there is here once the sun starts to go down."

Russ chuckled and stepped out of the way. "Why don't you come in then? Supper's just about ready."

His house smelled like roasting meat, chili peppers, and paprika. My stomach rumbled.

I left my shoes by the door. My smiley face socks were at least a little less embarrassing than the monkey socks I'd been wearing yesterday, and I cared a lot less about Russ seeing my silly socks than Mark. Russ was old enough to be my father.

Russ came out of the kitchen with his arms full. "Supper will be a few minutes still. I didn't remember to ask what you'd like to drink so I grabbed one of everything that I had in my fridge."

One of everything turned out to be a bottle of spring water, a can of some sort of generic diet soda, an orange juice box, and a bottle of Beaver Tail beer. It must be a local favorite.

I twisted the cap off the water. "I found a contract while I was going through Uncle Stan's papers that I wanted to ask you about."

I slid the business partnership papers across the table.

Russ glanced at them and rubbed the back of his neck. "I was wondering if you'd eventually come across those."

"Why didn't you tell me right away? I feel like a jerk for talking about all my big plans of learning the business when you'd planned for this to be your business, yours and Uncle Stan's."

Russ pushed the papers back toward me with two fingers. "Did you look at the date?"

I hadn't. I snuck a peek. The agreement had originally been drafted six weeks ago, plenty of time for them to have finalized it all before Uncle Stan's death. "So his death wasn't what stopped the process."

"No," Russ said. "It wasn't."

He didn't offer any more. The lawyer part of my brain said I needed to probe further. That there was information here that could speak to Uncle Stan's death.

But I didn't believe for a second that Russ would have killed my uncle. They'd been best friends. Almost business partners. And Mark had vouched for him.

Don't be naïve, Nicole, the lawyerly part of my brain said. *You know anyone can be a killer given the right circumstances. And people lie all the time.*

True. Mark hadn't exactly been forthcoming about a lot of things. Well, one thing. But it was one very important thing if he wanted to do date-like activities and confuse me about his intensions.

I licked my dry lips. "Do you mind telling me why?"

Russ jabbed the straw into the juice box and slurped out some juice. It was a weird sight. The box vanished inside his meaty fist. "I'd rather not, but I also don't want you thinking I had a reason to kill Stan. I know you haven't stopped digging."

Oops. I twisted my hands together in my lap. "Am I that easy to read?"

Russ shook his head. "It's a small town, remember. Word gets around."

Mark had said almost the same thing. I'd have to keep that in mind. Maybe it was my city-girl mentality, but I liked at least some parts of my private business to stay private. "So why didn't you finalize the partnership?"

"I was involved in something your uncle didn't approve of." Russ sucked the last of the juice from the juice box and crushed it. "Nothing illegal or anything like that, but we had a blow-up over it. We couldn't finish the agreement because we weren't even talking when he died."

Holy cheese and rice. I chugged some of my water to help hide my face. He might have said I wasn't easy to read, but right now my emotions were probably splattering everywhere.

Russ claimed he'd told me because he didn't want me thinking he'd had anything to do with Uncle Stan's death, but it sounded an awful lot like he had a motive.

Russ sighed and I choked on a bit of water. He waited until I stopped hacking.

"This time you were easy to read," he said.

Yup, I'd figured as much. "It doesn't sound the greatest admitting to having an argument that serious with someone shortly before they were murdered."

"Nope. Which is why I didn't blurt it out the first day you started nosing around."

A timer went off in the kitchen.

Russ got up. "Hang on a sec. That'll be the pork roast."

An image of Russ grabbing a carving knife and disposing of me as well flashed across my mind. I shook my head. Some parts of my personality at least made me well-suited to being a lawyer. I apparently did suspect everyone.

Russ returned with a massive serving platter filled with tender-looking pork, potatoes, and carrots. He laid it in the middle of the table.

I eyed him sideways. "You always cook a meal for eight, or were you expecting someone else tonight?"

He laughed. "I hate cooking, so I make enough for leftovers."

His maple-glazed pork roast had the perfect amount of sweetness and zing. It didn't overwhelm my taste buds with sugar. We spent the next few minutes filling our stomachs and talking about more pleasant things.

But I couldn't let it go. "It'd help me a lot if you explained this a bit more."

He eased his chair back from the table. "What good would it do me to kill Stan when we didn't have the agreement signed yet?"

He didn't sound angry at all, not like the first time. Maybe it was because I was only asking about him and not about other people.

"I certainly don't benefit at all from his death now." Russ stacked our bowls. "And you might as easily have come up here and fired me, bringing in your own people. Or sold the place and left me working for someone who'd mismanage it and run it into the ground. I'd be an idiot to kill Stan with no signatures on that paper."

"Most people aren't thinking clearly when they kill someone. You might have done it out of anger."

He shook his head and shrugged. "Ask around town about me then. Anyone who knows me'll tell you it'd take a whole lot more than that to make me kill anyone, let alone Stan. Dessert?"

I'd let the matter drop for now. I wasn't any more convinced than when the conversation started that Russ killed Uncle Stan.

But tomorrow, when I picked up my car and swung by to get Fay for my tour, I'd see what she knew about what Russ and Uncle Stan could have disagreed about strongly enough that it would make best friends not speak to each other for weeks.

Chapter 11

When Tony at Quantum Mechanics handed me my car keys, I actually considered kissing the hood of my car. Or him. Or both.

Then I reminded myself that gossip travels faster than electricity in this town. I took the keys and drove toward Fay's house.

My phone rang with a number I didn't recognize. I put it through my car's Bluetooth. "Nicole Fitzhenry-Dawes."

"This is Chief Carl Wilson."

My hands shook a little, and I tightened them around the wheel. Maybe I wouldn't have to keep investigating. Maybe he'd solved the case. "Do you have news on my uncle's murder?"

"What?" Confusion laced his words. "Oh. That. No, I'm calling because you were supposed to pick Fay up to tour Fair Haven."

My GPS told me to turn left. "I'm on my way, so if she was worried, I'll be there in just a minute. It took longer to get my car than I thought it would."

"Actually, I'm calling because Fay isn't feeling well enough to go out today. You'll have to reschedule."

Before I could ask him if there was anything I could do for her, he hung up. Which was kind of rude.

I kept following the GPS directions. I was so close to their house now that I might as well swing by. Fay couldn't go out, but perhaps she wanted some company or a gofer to pick up something for her. It must be horrible to be trapped in your home, scared and frustrated.

I parked in their driveway and made my way up to the front door.

Chief Wilson's police cruiser sat in the driveway beside my car, so I should be okay to ring the bell. If it hadn't been here, I might have stuck my head in the door and asked Fay if I could come in so she wouldn't have to get up.

I reached for the doorbell, and the door swung open.

Chief Wilson's mouth drooped and he frowned. He was dressed in his uniform.

I held up a hand. "I know you said she's not feeling up to taking a ride around town, but I wanted to see if there was some way I could help."

He glanced back over his shoulder. "I don't want her tired out by—"

"Ask her in," a strained version of Fay's voice said from somewhere behind him. "Then you don't have to feel guilty about leaving me to go to work."

Chief Wilson grunted and stepped aside.

Once I was inside, I spotted Fay in the living room recliner, her feet up and what looked like a handmade quilt spread over her. Her face had a distinctive gray pallor.

I knelt beside her chair and took one of her hands in mine. It was like holding ice. I chuffed her hand a little to warm it up. "I know I don't like to be alone when I'm not feeling well. I thought you might be the same."

She blinked rapidly. "I hate feeling this way."

Chief Wilson kissed Fay on the forehead. "I'll be home at the usual time."

She nodded.

His heavy footsteps faded away, and the click of the front door finally muffled them completely.

I got to my feet. "How about something warm to drink? Tea?"

"Chamomile." Fay leaned her head back. "I don't want to risk anything with caffeine. I probably brought this on myself. I had a second cup of coffee this morning. I should know better." She tapped her chest gently. "Caffeine and heart conditions don't mix."

I'd guessed as much when I found only decaf in Uncle Stan's cupboards this morning. I needed to make a grocery run later today and stock up since I planned to stay for a while. A girl cannot live on decaf alone. At least not this girl.

I put her kettle on the stove. Did you add something to herbal teas or drink them straight? "Milk and sugar?" I called back.

Fay's laugh told me I had it all wrong. "Honey and lemon. There should be a lemon in the fridge."

I stuck my head in her fridge and poked around in search of the lemon. A bottle toppled over and I caught it before it rolled off the shelf. Beaver's Tail beer again. If it was any good, I should buy a six-pack to take home to my dad, help smooth things over. He loved trying out regional beers from microbreweries.

I carried the bottle out into the living room and held it up. "Is this any good?"

Fay made a face. "Oh heavens no. You don't want to drink that. It's awful stuff. The only people who actually drink it are tourists looking for the best buzz they can get without breaking the law."

My mind spun with questions. If this beer was so bad that only tourists drank it, then why did Uncle Stan, Russ, and Carl all have bottles in their fridge? Someone had planted the bottles in Uncle Stan's fridge, and I had to assume the only person with a reason to do that would be the person who forced him to drink it.

Right now, I didn't like where the options for who that person was were pointing.

I made sure my voice came out level and casual. "Do you keep it in your fridge as a conversation piece then?"

Fay tucked her blanket in more tightly around her legs. "Carl bought a few six-packs during the investigation. He couldn't bring home any logged in as actual evidence, but he wanted to do some extra research into the contents himself."

The kettle whistled. I ducked back into the kitchen, prepared Fay's tea, and put some of the sugar cookies from the other day onto a plate as well in case she felt like a snack.

After I set her up with a TV table, I dropped onto the seat of the couch nearest her. "Your husband was investigating beer?"

Fay actually smiled. Talking did seem to be taking her mind off of how poorly she felt. Which was a good thing, since otherwise I wouldn't have felt right about pestering her. When I'd made my original plan to question her about the small town gossip surrounding Russ and Uncle Stan's falling out, I hadn't counted on her health taking a dip.

"He was investigating Beaver Tail Brewery," Fay said. "Someone accused them of producing beer with a dangerously high caffeine content. Since this is a tourist town, Carl didn't want to take any chances. He shut them down until he could be sure the beer was safe."

I crossed my legs to keep from bouncing on my seat like a little kid. On my first day in town, hadn't someone at The Chop Shop been talking about a local brewer who was in trouble with the law again? I didn't technically have a connection to Uncle Stan yet, so I'd need more information, but a man with a history of legal trouble seemed like someone it would be reasonable to check out. And I liked thinking about him as a suspect a lot more than I liked thinking about Russ as a suspect.

It was the middle of the afternoon by the time I left Fay and headed for The Chop Shop. If the small-town gossip mill was as well-developed as everyone claimed it was, I should be able to find out at least a bit of useful information about Beaver Tail Brewers there before I went barging up to the owner and asking questions about his relationship with Uncle Stan.

I paused outside The Chop Shop's doorway. The only problem with this plan was that it required me to have my hair cut. I kept my hair long for a reason. It had zero volume, and that meant my two favorite hairstyles were ponytails and a French twist. If I cut it off, I'd be out of luck.

But hair grew back. People didn't.

I pushed open the door. The same little boy as before camped out in the corner. Today's toys were a multi-colored collection of blocks that he seemed to be building into a fort.

Unlike the first day I'd come, the place seemed deserted.

"You're too late," the little boy said. "Today is close-early day."

Most hairdressers I knew stayed closed on Mondays since they were open Saturdays, but I'd never heard of one closing early on Tuesdays. "What's close-early day?"

His tongue stuck out a little as he worked to balance another brick on a precariously high corner tower. "When tourists aren't coming in, we close early on Tuesdays because all the regular customers go to Bingo at five o'clock."

I swallowed down a little snort. "Do you think your mom would make an exception for me?"

It wasn't exactly what I'd hoped for, but maybe this would actually work out better. I wouldn't have the benefit of all the local gossips, but I could talk one-on-one with Liz, and perhaps she'd be more open with her opinions than she would have been in a group setting.

"I think I can make an exception just this once," Liz's voice said from behind me.

I tried to turn around, but only managed to lose my balance and flop down onto my bottom. Liz covered her mouth with her hand.

I picked myself up and brushed off my bottom. "It's okay. You can laugh. I'm pretty much the clumsiest person on the planet, much to my mother's dismay and embarrassment."

Liz moved her hand, revealing a grin. "Let me lock the door and switch the sign so I don't end up with any more walk-ins on close-early day." She winked at me. "Derek looks forward to close-early day because we have time to play before supper."

Liz washed my hair and set me up in a chair while we made the regular get-to-know-you small talk.

"So what would you like done today?" she finally asked.

I glanced at her reflection in the mirror in front of me. She had the kind of hair I'd always wanted—dark, thick, and curly. My own hair was more like a flattened mouse. "I'd ask if you could give me more body and curl, but I'd been there before and it was a disaster."

"One thing I've discovered since becoming a stylist is that women with straight hair envy women with curly hair, and women with curly hair envy women with straight hair." She caught my gaze in the mirror. "We're never happy just being us. Somehow I don't think guys have these problems."

"Probably not," I said.

"How about you trust me to give you a cut that'll look great on you?"

I don't know that I'd ever trusted any hairdresser to be able to do that, but nothing she could do would be

worse than the other cuts I'd had before. The last stylist convinced me that I needed a change in color. Not
everyone looks good as a blonde, let me tell you.

But what I said was, "Sure. I'll trust you."

Liz set to work. "So I hear you've decided to stay in
Fair Haven."

The first long strand of hair fell to the ground and I
closed my eyes. It was now or never to start poking
around. "I'm considering it. I'm a little concerned
about how much crime there might be. I'm single, so
I'd be living alone out on the edge of town."

Liz let out a puff of air. "Don't believe everything
you hear about tourist towns. You're probably safer
here than you are in whatever city you came from."

Liz's scissors fell silent.

I opened my eyes. She was looking at my hair with
the same expression Derek had worn when trying to
balance that last block, even down to the tip of her
tongue peeking out between her lips.

I stayed perfectly still. "I've been hearing rumors
about a brewery near here and problems with the police."

"That's just Jason." Her scissors went to work
again, and she glanced over at where Derek played.
"Jason and I dated in high school. That's how I ended
up a single mom. He's an idiot, but he's otherwise
harmless."

If I'd actually been worried about crime in Fair Haven, that pronouncement would have made me happy.

But *harmless* wasn't how I was hoping to hear him described. If he was harmless and hadn't been behind Uncle Stan's murder, than that left me back with Russ again.

Then again, I couldn't simply take Liz's word for it. Her past history with him might be clouding her judgment. "You're sure? I heard he had a history of violence."

Hopefully she wouldn't ask me who I'd heard it from since I highly doubted making up a person for my made up lie would work.

"That was just the one time. He took a crowbar to my car. But it worked out for me in the end because I got full custody of Derek."

She swiveled my chair around so I wasn't facing the mirror and turned on the blow dryer, effectively stopping any conversation, but what I'd heard was enough. Jason the Brewer was back on my list of suspects.

After a few minutes, Liz spun me back around. "What do you think?"

I blinked and rubbed my eyes. That was not my hair. It couldn't possibly be my hair. It looked...amazing. It had body. "Holy crap. How'd you do that?"

Liz grinned. "I'll write down the instructions for you. Best part is that it shouldn't take you more than five minutes to style when you get out of the shower."

I drove back to Uncle Stan's house—now my house—trying not to think about what Mark would say if he could see me now. Then I dove back into sorting through Uncle Stan's belongings.

I must have fallen asleep because I woke up with a kink in my neck, a queasy stomach, and smelling natural gas.

Chapter 12

I stumbled to my feet, but the world spun around me and my stomach rolled. Every step felt like the floor tipped under me in a different direction.

How long had I been breathing this in? The smell, like a mix of rotten eggs and skunk, was strong, but didn't they make it that way on purpose so you'd know in time if you had a leak? What happened to Uncle Stan's carbon monoxide detectors? Back when he lived in Virginia, he was the kind of man who changed his fire alarm batteries with the twice-yearly time change and had not one but two carbon monoxide detectors in his thousand-square-foot apartment.

I focused on dragging my mind back from the rabbit trails it wanted to run down. Had to be the effect of the gas.

I couldn't remember if I was supposed to open a window if I smelled gas or if I was supposed to leave the house and call the gas company. My brain felt fuzzy, like someone took an eraser to it. I picked up my purse and headed for the stairs. I wasn't going to risk taking the time to open a window. I needed to get out.

I tripped over my own feet and caught myself on the railing, inches from tumbling head-first down the stairs.

One step at a time. I reached the bottom.

It was dark outside. Dark in the house. But I didn't dare turn on any lights.

I ran my shin into something, and pain spiraled up my leg.

The door had to be somewhere to the left. I limped toward it and groped around until I located the doorknob. It didn't budge.

My heart punched up into my throat. *Don't let it be stuck. Don't let it be stuck.*

I tugged again, straining all the muscles in my back. Wait. It couldn't be stuck. I'd come in through this door a few hours ago. Had I locked it?

I felt for the lock switch and turned it. I wrenched the knob again. This time the door flew open easily and I half raced, half fell out the door and into the yard. I left the door hanging open behind me.

I gulped in breaths of air so cold it burned down into my lungs. My coat was inside, but I wasn't going back for it.

I glanced behind me, barely able to make out the bulk of the house. Dark clouds blocked out all but the tiniest sliver of light from the moon.

My head started to clear, and my teeth chattered. I still felt too close. I backed up right to the edge of the trees and took out my phone, dialing 9-1-1.

The dispatcher assured me she was sending help. She wanted me to stay on the line, but my hands shook so hard I couldn't hold the phone. I accidentally dropped it, and the call disconnected.

The eerie darkness closed in on me, along with a sense of absolute vulnerability. I wrapped my arms around my waist. Somehow I needed to focus my mind on something other than the fact that I could have died and that I was alone out here. Nothing came to mind, so I recited the Constitution just to hear my own voice.

In less than five minutes, flashing lights zoomed up the drive way, and I waved an arm at the approaching vehicles. Soon I was wrapped in a blanket in the back of an ambulance, while a paramedic examined me.

"You're really lucky," he said. "Most people who have a leak like this while they're sleeping never wake up."

Thanks. As if I wasn't already freaked out enough. "Am I okay then?"

"You're free to go."

I carefully climbed down from the ambulance. He might say I was fine, but my legs still felt like loose Jell-O. I tottered my way over to the police cruiser.

The man next to it talking to a representative from the gas company wasn't Chief Wilson, but I couldn't expect the man to work 24/7 even if he was the chief of police. In the strange alternating light cast by his cruiser, I couldn't get a solid look at this officer's features. I thought he was closer to my age than Chief Wilson's—and built like a brick wall.

"Do they know yet what caused the leak?" I asked.

The officer turned toward me and motioned the gas company employee forward.

"Not yet, ma'am," the man said. "There doesn't seem to be an obvious leak. We've turned the gas off for now, but it won't be safe for you to stay here until we've located the cause. You're certain you didn't leave a burner on the stove? Or something else that could have accidentally blown out and caused a false leak?"

"I didn't turn anything on when I came home today."

"And it didn't smell like gas when you arrived home?"

I hoped my look clearly said *I'm not that stupid.* "I wouldn't have gone in if it had."

The man scratched his head. "One other thing, ma'am. Your carbon monoxide detector was unplugged. You should really be more careful about that."

I put it at the top of my mental list to check when I was able to go back into the house. It was a bit irksome that everyone was looking at me as if I were at fault. I'd been in this town for barely a week, and I hadn't even had time to look in all the closets in the house, let alone know if something was broken. For all I knew, I might turn on a tap tomorrow and start a flood. I added *Check the fire alarm batteries* to my mental list as well. At least then if the house did accidentally catch fire, no one could blame me.

The officer thanked the natural gas employee, and the man returned to the house, where other men were now crawling around my home like ants.

The officer scratched his chin. "How about you take a seat in the car with me? I have a few questions I need to ask."

I squinted at where his nametag should be, but it was too dark out even with all the emergency lights to read it. "I don't have to get in the back, do I?"

He chuckled. "You're not under arrest, so no. You can sit up front with me."

He opened the passenger door and I climbed inside. Even up front, the car smelled like stale coffee, urine, and vomit. I breathed through my mouth and thanked Uncle Stan's God that the officer hadn't put me in the back. I might have had to burn my clothes, and at present, they were the only set I had access to.

The officer slid in behind the wheel, turned on the car, and adjusted the heat.

"Thank you," I said.

"You looked awfully cold even wrapped up in that blanket." He shifted slightly so that he was angled toward me. "When something like this happens, we have to check into things, you understand?"

I nodded. I understood that they had to check into it, anyway. I had no idea what questions he might need to ask. Two tiny balls of tension formed beneath my shoulder blades.

"You haven't been feeling suicidal lately?"

To quote Velma from the *Scooby-Doo* cartoons I watched as a kid, *Jinkies!* What kind of person tries to kill themselves with a gas leak? Had anyone ever actually done that? I could see now why he led into this by suggesting he had to ask these questions. "No, sir. I'd much rather be alive than dead. If I'd wanted to kill myself, I would have stayed in the house."

He gave what I interpreted as an apologetic shrug. "And have you been having any money troubles lately?"

What happened to the small town gossip chain? "None. I just inherited from my uncle."

This time he smiled. "I know. I've heard the story, but they make us ask these things in case you tried to blow up your house and collect the insurance money."

I assumed Uncle Stan had home insurance—he liked to be prepared for every contingency—but I hadn't run across the policy yet. "Well, I can put you in touch with whoever you might need to reach to check on my financials, if you'd like."

"No need. Like I said, this is routine. I expect once they can check the place over again in the light, they'll find a faulty valve or some such."

He must not realize I was a lawyer. I knew perfectly well that there was no such thing as *routine questions*. If I answered in a way that sent up any red flags for him, everything I said would matter. Thankfully, I really *didn't* have anything to hide.

He stopped jotting notes and flipped the page in his notepad. "And do you know of anyone who might wish to harm you?"

My mouth went dry. If I'd started to ask too many questions to or about Uncle Stan's killer, could this "leak" be an attempt to stop me? That felt melodramatic to even think it, but the officer wouldn't have asked me if it wasn't a possibility.

"Ma'am?"

I blinked and focused on his face. "Sorry. I don't know about that last one. Is it alright if I answer with a maybe?"

His body language went from casual to practiced casual. A little tighter in the shoulder muscles. His movements a little slower. "If someone might have been trying to hurt you, who do you think it was?"

Last night I'd quizzed Russ on his argument with Uncle Stan, and this afternoon I'd been prying into the business of Jason the brewer. Liz might have claimed he was her ex, but that didn't mean he was or that they didn't still talk. They had a child together, after all.

Heck, even Derek could have said something to his dad about me asking after him.

My questions could have made either of the two men nervous if they were the killer, but nervous enough to try to kill me, too? As far as I knew, I hadn't uncovered anything solid enough to justify that, but if this had been an attack on me, it meant I'd stumbled on some of the pieces that could lead me there.

Russ' words about how even an unfounded suspicion could hurt a person's livelihood in this town came back to me. Assuming for a moment that one of the two men was the killer, that meant the other was innocent and didn't deserve a police investigation into their life.

"I'm not sure," I said. "But someone killed my Uncle Stan a week ago. I've been showing curiosity into the circumstances of his death. It's possible his murderer felt threatened."

The officer rubbed under the rim of his hat. "I wish you'd told me this right away. I'd have had the men from the gas company turn off the gas and then move away until we'd had a chance to check for fingerprints or other signs of forced entry."

If someone had tried to kill me, they would have worn gloves. Whoever this killer was, they were smart. They'd have had to be to kill Uncle Stan in the first place and then cover it up so nicely. The gas company probably wouldn't be able to prove whether this leak was accidental or intentional.

They were smart, and it was possible they wanted to kill me.

My stomach rolled and turned my throat into a ball of fire. I grabbed the car door handle and concentrated on the coolness of the plastic. My therapist called it grounding. Focusing on something solid in my environment was supposed to short-circuit my brain and prevent it from flicking the hyperventilate-or-pass-out switch.

But having the officer there staring at me wasn't helping.

I needed to be alone for a minute or I was going to slide right into a full-blown panic attack. "Since I can't stay here tonight, am I able to at least go back inside long enough to collect my things?"

"I'll check with the gas company, but I don't see why not."

The officer left.

I drew in a few deep diaphragm breaths. It was possible someone had actually tried to kill me. The panic faded away and something hotter and stronger replaced it. Something that felt a lot like fury.

If whoever had killed Uncle Stan thought they could kill me or scare me away, they'd made a major miscalculation.

Chapter 13

The next morning, I cradled a cup of The Sunburnt Arm's awful coffee between my hands. I'd slept as late as I could, and so the coffee was particularly strong and a little stale. If I stayed here long enough, I might actually develop a taste for the stuff.

I released the cup and tapped my phone on the table. If last night was an attack, it meant I was on the right track. Now more than ever, I wanted to talk to Jason the brewer.

But I'm not stupid. And I'm definitely not reckless. Anxiety issues and risk-taking don't exactly go together.

So if someone was willing to blow me up and my new home with me, I needed to be careful. I couldn't go talk to Jason alone. Fay was too sick to go with me. Russ didn't think I should be investigating in the first place, and I had to consider him a real suspect. My gas "leak" happened only a day after I'd found out that Russ and Uncle Stan had a big enough argument to prevent them from finalizing their business partnership. Plus Russ had easy access to Uncle Stan's house and a key to get in.

That left Mark as my crime-solving partner.

My call went to voicemail, and I left a message.

My phone rang less than five minutes later, showing Mark's number on the screen. I glanced around the room, to make sure it was still empty, and answered. I filled Mark in on everything that had happened in the past day.

A few seconds of silence followed, then a whoosh of air like someone letting out a breath. "Have you heard from the gas company yet today?"

"Nothing yet."

"So it could still have been an accident?"

"It's possible."

"And what do you plan to do if it turns out it wasn't an accident?" His words had a cautious edge to them, like he was weighing each one before speaking it.

"I'm going to keep investigating, whether it was an accident or not."

"Nikki—"

"If I can get a little more evidence, enough to point to a clear suspect, then I can take it to Chief Wilson and let them handle the rest. But I can't stop now. This could mean I'm close."

Muffled voices carried over the phone, and his reply was equally garbled, as if he'd placed his hand over it. I braved another sip of coffee. One of the things Fay had promised to show me during our canceled tour was someplace to buy a good cup of coffee. I could have really used that information right about now.

"You're not still staying at your uncle's house?" Mark said, his voice clear again.

"I've moved back in to The Sunburnt Arms." I shifted my phone to the other ear. "Listen, the reason I'm calling is that I know it's not safe to go asking around by myself anymore and I want to drive out to Beaver Tail Brewery to talk to Jason. I was hoping you'd come along."

"As your bodyguard?" There was a hint of teasing in his tone now at least.

"Something like that, yeah. Bodyguard. Medical expert."

"I don't think you should keep investigating this."

The teasing note was gone again.

My own smile faded. "I know, but I have to. We've already had this discussion. Please come with me. I don't want to go alone."

It was the truth, but I'd implied that I would go with or without him, which of course I wouldn't. The twinge in my stomach felt an awful lot like guilt over manipulating him.

The line still sat silent except for the sound of quiet breathing.

"Please," I said again.

He sighed. "I'm at work right now, but I'll pick you up around three-thirty."

Since I couldn't go back to work sorting through Uncle Stan's belongings and Mark wouldn't be by until the afternoon, I decided to use the time to make an essential purchase—a flashlight. Seemed like a necessity in this weird streetlightless town. To be fair, they did have streetlights in the town proper. Unfortunately for me, those ended long before my new home. Uncle Stan must have a flashlight somewhere, but I wasn't taking any chances. The dark out at Sugarwood was creepy, and it got dark here before supper.

I pulled into the parking lot and found a spot as close to the front door as possible. The hardware store seemed like a holdout in the business-naming scheme of the rest of the town, which lent credence to my theory that any business catering to the locals stuck to stating what they did. The large blue-and-white sign read DAD'S HARDWARE STORE. And in smaller letters underneath was NUTZ, BOLTZ, TOOLS, ETC. The misspelling of *nuts* and *bolts* might have been accidental, but I suspected it was an intentional nose thumb at the cutesy names all around them.

The wind bit my cheeks as soon as I stepped out of my car. I tucked my face down low into my coat collar and jogged across the parking lot. My phone vibrated in my purse, but I waited until I ducked inside the door to pull it out. It was Fay.

I tapped the screen. "Hey, you must be a mind reader. I was going to call you today to see how you were feeling."

"A bit better. I've even had enough energy this morning to work on the layout for the flyers I'm doing for Carl's upcoming run for sheriff."

She'd been excited the day before when she told me about Chief Wilson's plans to run for sheriff at the next election, and her voice did sound less strained than yesterday, but the thought of her working on anything—even something she was enthusiastic about—after how weak she'd been sent a twinge of worry through me. "Are you sure you shouldn't be resting instead?"

"Carl said the same thing. He wanted to hire someone for it, but I used to be a graphic designer, and it's nice to feel useful."

"Just promise me you won't overdo it."

"Promise. But I called to ask—"

Dead air filled the line.

My heart slammed into my rib cage, then my phone chirped. I let out a long breath. Nothing had happened to Fay. The call simply dropped. This place had the most random tiny dead zone pockets. I'd had a full signal in the front of the store, but now no signal at all.

I quickly chose a medium-sized flashlight. The lens wasn't quite as large as a car headlight, but it wasn't far off, either. Exactly what I wanted.

I headed back to the front of the store. The signal on my phone picked up again, and I dialed Fay back.

"One of the endearing quirks of Fair Haven," Fay said. "You'll eventually figure out where the pockets are."

I set the flashlight on the checkout counter. "It makes my fingers twitch."

Fay laughed. "When we got disconnected, I was trying to ask how you're doing." The laughter was gone from her voice, a strained tone had replaced it. "I heard about last night."

The last thing she needed was to be worrying about me. The best way to set her mind at ease was probably to show her I was fine. And I could help her out in the process. "How about I grab us some lunch, and I'll come by and tell you about it and you can show me those flyers?"

"Do you drink Beaver's Tail beer?" I asked Mark as we pulled out of The Sunburnt Arms' parking lot at precisely 3:30.

He made a face. An actual face like a kid asked to eat a plate full of broccoli.

It was absolutely adorable.

"Not a chance," he said. "It tastes like dirty socks."

I couldn't help myself. "You've tasted dirty socks before?"

Only it turned out that he had, on a dare in college.

We spent the rest of the drive talking about where we'd gone to school. I wanted to ask if he'd met his wife at college, to try to wheedle more information out of him about whether or not they were still together, but we pulled into the Beaver's Tail Brewery parking lot before I could.

Only one other car, a beat-up-looking Honda with rust on the bumper, sat in the parking lot. A big red-and-white CLOSED sign hung in the window.

"When was this investigation?" I asked.

"A couple months ago or so. I'm not sure exactly. I wasn't the one who ran the tests, so I'd only heard about the investigation in passing before you brought it up today."

We walked across the gravel lot, and I tugged on the door. Even though the sign said the shop was closed, it wasn't locked.

I stuck my head in the door. The place smelled like yeast and pine-scented cleaner. "Hello?"

A man came from the back room, wiping his hands on a towel. Between his raggedy blond hair, stubble, and lean build, he looked a bit like a hungry coyote.

And based on his sallow skin and the dark circles under his eyes, like someone who took in most of his daily calories through sampling his own wares.

"Welcome to Beaver's Tail Brewery. I'm Jason Wood, owner." He balled up the towel. "I can give you a tour if you'd like, but we're not open for sales right now."

If he thought we were tourists, maybe I could play that angle for a little bit. "A tour sounds great, but why can't we buy anything?"

I stepped through the doorway. Moving in gave me a better look at the layout of the store showroom. Natural wood shelves lined the walls and were filled floor to ceiling with six-packs. He didn't seem to sell cases or individual bottles. It might have been a production thing or a marketing thing. I didn't know enough about microbreweries to know.

Artfully hand-painted signs hung over the different varieties—five total. The sign over the bottles that matched the ones I'd seen in Uncle Stan's house, as well as in Russ' and Fay's fridges, declared it their most popular beer, with subtle notes of banana. Banana-coffee beer sounded about as appealing as the dirty sock from Mark's story, but based on what I'd learned from Fay, people didn't exactly drink the stuff for the taste.

Mark followed me in, and the door swooshed shut behind him.

Jason's gaze bounced to him and he frowned. "I know you're not here for a tour. What's this really about?"

I cringed. Right. Small town. Most people knew each other, and Mark's connection to Cavanaugh Funeral Home probably meant more people knew him than didn't. I might have had a better chance if I had come alone.

Time for a new tactic. I extended my hand. "Nicole Fitzhenry-Dawes. I just moved to town, and I'm trying to familiarize myself with all the local establishments."

Jason let fly a few choice curse words. "Dawes. Like Stan Dawes?"

I guess that answered the question of whether they'd ever met. "I'm his niece."

"I oughtta throw you out. I'll be lucky if I can keep from going bankrupt thanks to your uncle."

A lawyer needs to be adaptable, my father always said. *You won't know for sure how a witness will react on the stand until it happens.*

Jason's open hatred for Uncle Stan certainly wasn't what I'd expected. My read on him was that if I defended Uncle Stan at all or sounded too much like I was grilling Jason to explain himself, he probably would kick us out. I'd leave knowing animosity existed, but not what caused it and whether Jason could have killed him.

The other tactic would leave me feeling like I needed a shower. I might be terrible at flirting, but I could do false sympathy like nobody's business.

"I didn't realize." I crossed the space between us and placed my hand on Jason's upper arm. I gave him my best remorseful look. "I'm really sorry my uncle caused problems for you. Everyone's been telling me about how much the tourists love your beers. It'd be a shame if you closed."

Jason flashed me a smarmy grin, and I caught a glimpse of the player he must have been back in high school. "I've been thinking of making up signs with my new slogan. *Best buzz you can get without getting arrested.*"

Fay had said that was why the tourists bought Jason's beer, but to hear it openly pitched that way made me want to gag.

Mark poked a six-pack on a shelf. The bottles inside clinked. "What, exactly, goes into this buzz-inducing beer?" His voice sounded the exact opposite of my ingratiating simper. His expression was stiff.

Jason stalked over to him and steadied the six-pack. "I have multiple recipes, but that's proprietary information, man."

Proprietary? That was an awfully big word for someone who Liz described as a harmless idiot.

He'd given himself away. At least to me. He was the type who could have pulled all A's in high school but chose to smoke outside the gym and get high on Friday nights instead. And that combination of intelligence and a willingness to circumvent the law made him dangerous.

He and Mark were still staring each other down like stags about to lock horns.

I wedged myself in between them. "But you said it's a legal buzz. Why would my uncle have a problem with that?"

The innocent baby-doll voice was straining my vocal cords, but I was clearly going to get further with him keeping it up than using Mark's unhelpful brute-force approach.

Jason slipped an arm around my waist and led me toward the door in the back that he'd come through when we first arrived. Up close, he had a sickeningly sweet smell not completely covered up by his cologne. "Stan got everyone all worked up about the caffeine content in my beer. He said it was high enough to cause heart problems even in people with healthy hearts. Something about spiking their heart rates. It was a load of bull."

My skin crawled under his touch. Literally crawled. I don't know how he couldn't feel it twitching. "But the police believed him."

"Yeah." He pushed open the door to the back room. Most of the shelves were empty. "They shut me down and confiscated a lot of my product. They even took containers of my ingredients for sampling, my hops, my caffeine powder. Then I got a call a few weeks later saying they'd cleared me. I'd told them all along—my beer's no more dangerous than a Jägerbomb."

If he'd been cleared, it diluted his possible motive some, but not entirely. He'd still been unable to earn a living from his business for however long, he was out the money for the product the police took, plus he'd be behind on his stock. That might be enough to send his business under even though he'd been cleared.

"Why are you still closed if you've been cleared?" Mark asked.

I jumped. I'd been so focused on trying to put the pieces together that I almost forgot he was there watching it all.

"I'm waiting for my liquor license to renew. The police are always out here checking to make sure I'm not illegally making sales before I have it." Jason glared at him. "It lapsed while they had me closed down, and I wasn't going to pay for months I wasn't using."

He might be a sleaze, but the more he talked, the more convinced I became that he was savvy as well. He had a motive. He'd probably found out about Uncle Stan's heart condition sometime during the accusations and investigation. And his beer was used as part of the murder weapon.

That last part didn't quite fit with the rest of the carefully planned crime, but maybe it was a Vizzini-like switch. He knew that anyone would assume he couldn't have been the killer because who would be stupid enough to use their own brand of beer? But did he know that I knew that he knew?

"I can see why you would have been angry with my uncle. If it'd been me, I would have wanted payback."

Jason pulled me in closer. "I'll let you make it up to me if you'd like. I wouldn't want the guilt to eat you up the way it looks like it did him."

Was that a come-on or a threat?

Mark made a noise in his throat that was somewhere between a choke and a growl.

I'd had enough of this, too. I twisted out of Jason's grip and tucked in close enough to Mark that my arm brushed his. "So where were you the night Stan died?"

Jason's eyes flashed from warm to cold. He clearly wasn't used to women playing him or turning him down. "Who cares where I was? The old man killed himself."

Now that he was angry, he was harder to read. I couldn't tell if his surprise was genuine or faked. "He's been murdered and the investigation into his death is back open."

Jason's fists clenched. "What is it with your family and wanting to shut me down? Is this some sort of a Baptist anti-drinking conspiracy?"

Did Uncle Stan go to a Baptist church? I didn't know all the denominations or what they stood for. Either way, I wasn't about to let him sidetrack me by trying to make this religious. Uncle Stan's faith had nothing to do with it. "All you have to do to get rid of me is tell me where you were that night."

"I was down at Hops, talking to Kevin Franklin about carrying my beer."

I gave him a syrupy-sweet smile. "Thank you." Jerk.

As soon as Mark and I were back out in the parking lot, I pulled out my phone and dialed Chief Wilson.

"For a lawyer, you're willing to make some pretty big leaps," Chief Wilson said. "You know that's not enough to arrest him on."

"Of course not." I climbed into the truck with Mark. "I'm not asking you to. I'm just hoping you'll check out his alibi."

"That's reasonable. If it falls through, it'll be a reason to dig a little deeper."

One thing had been eating at me. Chief Wilson might be the person who could give me the answer. "My uncle wasn't the type of man to run around making accusations that could hurt people without evidence. Do you know why he was so convinced Jason's beer was dangerous?"

"Russ had a scare with his heart, and you know how Stan liked to help people. Russ didn't want to point fingers, but he finally told your uncle that he'd been drinking Beaver's Tail beer when it happened."

That must have been before their falling out. It wasn't likely the two were connected, but Russ wasn't exactly forthcoming about the details around his argument with Uncle Stan. "Thanks, Chief."

"Yeah, yeah. But Nicole?"

"Yes."

"You got to stop trying to investigate this. That gas leak at your house last night was most likely a warning. I don't want to see you get yourself killed."

If Jason turned out to be the killer, there wouldn't be much more to investigate. "Let me know if Jason's alibi holds up. If it doesn't, I might not need to investigate anymore."

We ended the call, though Chief Wilson's grumbled goodbye made it clear he wasn't happy with my answer. I snuggled back in Mark's seat. I shot him a triumphant smile, but it faded out almost before it hit my lips.

His hands gripped the wheel like he was trying to strangle it. And he looked angry.

Chapter 14

Mark's death-hold on the steering wheel turned his knuckles white. "What was that about?"

He was right. I shouldn't have antagonized Chief Wilson. "I know I should have told him I'd stop nosing around, but that would have been lying."

"Not that." He squeezed the words out between gritted teeth. "The flirting."

He didn't think...I laughed. "That wasn't flirting. I'm the world's worst flirt."

"You looked pretty good at it to me."

"I'm telling you, that wasn't flirting. That was plying a witness. With someone like Jason, it's the only way to get the information you want."

He looked at me sidelong and quirked an eyebrow in an I'm-not-buying-it expression.

I fisted my hands on the seat beside my legs. Why was I even arguing this with him? It's not like he was my boyfriend. I could darn well flirt with whoever I wanted. He had zero right to be jealous, especially given the wedding ring on his hand.

And I hadn't even been flirting!

We drove in silence for five minutes while I scowled out the window. We passed The Chop Shop for the second time.

"Why are we driving in circles?"

Mark's hands loosened on the wheel. "Because I was a jerk, and I'm trying to figure out how to apologize before I drop you off. I'm not good at this stuff."

We were both speaking English, but it felt like different dialects. "At apologizing?"

"At women. At people, really. Grant was always the people person. I'm better with data and facts. There's a right and a wrong answer with numbers. It's one of the reasons I became an ME rather than a GP or a surgeon. Cadavers don't care about your people skills."

I smoothed my palms out onto my thighs and chewed on my bottom lip. He seemed so self-assured that I'd assumed he was equally confident inside. "Well, how about I give you a little lesson then?"

"It's a trap," he said softly in a passable imitation of Admiral Ackbar from *Star Wars*.

I cracked up, and we'd passed The Chop Shop a third time before I caught my breath. "No trap. Promise." I crossed my heart.

He still looked skeptical. "Go ahead."

"This doesn't apply to all women, but if I were flirting, you'd know it because it would bear a frightening resemblance to a duck trying to perform slapstick comedy. I can work a witness because it's like acting. It's not the real me. But flirting needs to be genuine, and it does not come naturally to me."

He turned both his dimple and his eyebrow quirk on me this time, and heat flooded my veins.

"I think you underestimate yourself," he said. "You had Jason pretty enthralled."

I shrugged. "One of the few parts of being a lawyer that I'm good at is reading people and convincing them to open up to me. It's too bad that's such a small part of the job."

"I have a hard time imagining you weren't good at all parts of your career."

Since he'd bared his vulnerable underbelly to me, it seemed only fair I share as well. "I appreciate the vote of confidence, but there's a reason I've never been allowed to take the lead on any case, even though I work for my parents. If you asked them, they'd probably say something diplomatic like I 'fail to inspire confidence in the jury.' The truth is I get queasy and start to stutter and repeat myself when I have to speak in front of a crowd. I even tried Toastmasters to practice my public speaking, and my nerves got worse. You notice I didn't speak at Uncle Stan's funeral?"

Mark nodded.

"Well, now you know why."

Instead of turning down the road leading to The Chop Shop again, Mark went straight this time, heading toward The Sunburnt Arms.

I wasn't quite ready to head back yet. "Could you take me out to Sugarwood instead? It's still early enough that I want to talk to Russ about a few things."

Mark pulled a U-turn at the next intersection. "Do you think he can give you a ride back, or do you want me to wait?"

I'd rather he waited, but it wasn't because Russ wouldn't offer me a ride back. It was because I liked spending time with him, argument aside. And that was precisely the reason I shouldn't ask him to stay.

Besides, I wanted to ask Russ about Uncle Stan's run-in with Jason the brewer, and I wasn't sure he'd open up if Mark stayed. Russ was so worried about rumors spreading around this town. I wasn't a member of the town, so I wasn't part of the small town gossip chain. Mark might be—I didn't know.

The only problem with meeting with Russ alone was whether it was safe and smart. As much as I thought Jason was the best suspect for Uncle Stan's murder, he did claim to have an alibi. If his alibi held, all signs would point back to Russ once again.

So what was I more afraid of—Russ turning out to be the killer and "silencing" me or spending more time with Mark, putting my heart at risk with a man who wasn't available?

I'd suffered having my heart stomped on before, and it was still beating. I couldn't say the same for what would happen if I ended up in the sights of Uncle Stan's killer all alone. "It'd be nice if you could stay."

I filled him in on what Chief Wilson told me about Russ' connection to the Uncle Stan–Jason showdown.

Mark tapped his fingers on the steering wheel. "Russ is a good man. I can't see him killing Stan, not for anything."

"I don't think so, either, but even if he isn't, his side of the story might add to Jason's motive or provide other information that would help us figure out who did kill my uncle."

"I've been Sancho Panza to your Don Quixote this long. I might as well see it through." He reached over and brushed my hair with his fingertips. "I like the new look, by the way."

A warm feeling cuddled inside my chest. I loved the way he made film and book references the same way I did and the way he looked at me made me actually feel beautiful. I growled at myself silently. You'd think I was a moony teenager with how impossible it seemed to be to keep myself from wanting more than friendship with him.

"Does that mean you think I'm tilting at wind-mills?" I said. Hiding behind flippancy seemed like a good way to go since my heart was still beating a little too fast.

Mark chuckled. "How about Tonto to your Lone Ranger then?"

"I like the sound of that much better."

I called Russ and made sure he was home, then told him I was going to pick up something for dinner and bring it by to thank him for supper the other night. Mark recommended we pick up three fish-and-chips dinners from A Salt & Battery since he'd eaten there with Russ before. He even paid, waving away my objections with the notion that he wanted to make up for snapping at me earlier.

The only way to describe Russ when he opened the front door for us was haggard. He waddled out of the way, his barrel-frame rocking a bit more than usual. Mark went into the dining room to lay out the food, but I touched Russ' arm.

"Are you sure you're up to having us by?"

The smile he gave me was still as warm as the first time we met. "It's nothing a good night's sleep won't cure. I was up last night worrying about a sick friend."

In any crime show, a "sick friend" was almost a cli-ché, but I believed it of Russ. I hadn't told him yet about my adventure last night. I opened my mouth to catch him up, then clamped my lips shut again. He claimed worry over a sick friend, but sabotaging my gas line then waiting around in the woods to see what happened would explain his fatigue all the same. Or his sleepless nights could be born of guilt out of killing his best friend and trying to kill me.

A shiver trailed down my body. Maybe it was a good thing I brought Mark after all. Just in case. I'd deal with my rampant paranoia later if I were imagining it all.

Between my newfound concern, Russ' fatigue, and Mark's lack of social skills showing themselves a bit more, dinner was fairly quiet.

When Russ pushed aside his empty take-out container, I knew I couldn't wait any longer. And this time I was simply going to come at it directly. We'd had enough talks about whether or not Uncle Stan had enemies that Russ shouldn't think anything of it when I brought up Jason.

"I wanted to talk to you about something we found out today." I popped my take-out container closed. "We took a ride out to Beaver's Tail Brewery."

The smile faded from Russ' face, and the skin under his eyes sagged down into folds. "And Jason made your uncle sound like a lunatic, I'd guess. Don't let anything he said bother you."

It hadn't occurred to me to question whether Uncle Stan had sound reasons for going after Jason. I knew him too well to think otherwise, but Russ wouldn't know that. After all, I'd never been down to visit while Uncle Stan was alive.

The idea of how to move this conversation forward hit me almost immediately. Sometimes I hated myself for how my brain worked, and this was one of those times. Russ handed me an easy way to open up the conversation about what really happened, and I knew myself well enough to know that I was going to exploit it. Perhaps I was more like my dad than like Uncle Stan after all.

I twisted my fingers together on top of the table. "I don't understand why he would have made those accusations. Chief Wilson said he personally investigated Uncle Stan's claims and couldn't find anything to support them. Jason's beer is safe for anyone without a pre-existing heart condition."

Mark shot me a glance. He had to know exactly what I was up to this time.

My stomach twisted a little. If he spent much more time around me, I wouldn't have to worry about how attractive I found him. My ability to deceive people when I went into my lawyer mode wasn't an admirable quality. In fact, it was one I'd hoped to leave behind if I stopped being a lawyer. I guess it was more deeply engrained in my personality than I thought.

Russ' shoulders sagged. "It was all my fault."

I put on my best *how so?* look. If I'd been born tall, thin, pretty, and non-klutzy, I might have been an actress.

"I'd taken some medication that must have raised my blood pressure. Then, when I exercised, I felt like I might be having a heart attack."

The hesitation before the word *exercised* was slight, but it was the kind of tell I'd been trained to pick up on. I logged it in my mind as a point to return to when Russ finished talking.

"I didn't want to call 9-1-1," he said, "and set the gossip mill running, so I called Stan. I knew he'd been a cardiologist before he came here, and I figured he'd be able to either help me or tell me if I had to call an ambulance."

"He called an ambulance," Mark said, a statement, not a question. It must have been what he would have done as well.

Russ nodded. "I couldn't admit to what had actually caused the heart problem, so when they asked me, I remembered the bottle of Beaver's Tail I'd had sitting in the fridge and the talk about it and I said I'd drunk a couple bottles."

"But it wasn't true?" I asked, wanting to keep him talking.

"It wasn't."

His earlier bull-headedness about not wanting to even suggest a name because it could hurt the person's reputation suddenly made sense. He didn't want to repeat his past mistakes. I could respect that. Not repeating mistakes a second time was harder than most people made it sound.

He didn't volunteer any more information.

I propped my elbows on the table and leaned forward. "Given the situation, I think you should tell me what was really going on and why you lied."

"Given the circumstances?" Russ turned the same shade of sickly gray that the winter sky up here seemed to look six days out of seven. "You think Jason killed Stan."

Crap. Way to be self-centered and insensitive. If I were flexible enough to literally kick myself under the table, I would have done it. I hadn't made the connection before I spoke, but if Russ were innocent, the way I wanted to believe he was, he'd feel guilty for Uncle Stan's death at Jason's hands. His lie had started the chain of events that resulted in Jason's murderous fury.

Russ ground his thumb into the palm of his opposite hand. "The exercise. It involved a married lady. I couldn't let that get out. It'd ruin her."

My mind was bouncing all over again. If Uncle Stan found out and threatened to expose the affair... It meant the killer might not be Jason after all. Russ' motive would grow even stronger and the woman he was sleeping with would have a motive as well.

Mark and I exchanged a glance. His face had a drawn, slightly panicked look, like he expected Russ to confess to murder any second. He might be the medical examiner, but he wasn't a law enforcement officer. He didn't actually arrest people or deal with criminals aside from testifying against the accused in court.

And all my experience with "bad guys" had been defending them.

Come to think of it, my expression right now might very well look as panicked as Mark's.

"Did Uncle Stan figure out the truth?" My voice had a strangled sound to it and was about an octave higher than it should have been.

Russ bobbed his head. "After the police finished their testing on all the stuff they took from Jason's place, it was obvious a single beer hadn't caused the blip with my heart. Stan was furious. Called me a liar flat-out and demanded to know what really happened."

"So you killed him to protect your lover?" Mark asked.

"Good God, no." Russ leaned forward. "I never told him her name. She doesn't even know he found out about it." He must have read the continued suspicion on both our faces because he pointed at me. "The partnership papers you found. We never signed them because Stan refused to move forward with the partnership unless I stopped seeing her. He said it wasn't right what I was doing and it'd be on his conscience if he didn't say something. I refused. That's the argument we had that I told you about. But we would have worked it out, and all the reasons I told you why I'd never kill Stan are still true. He was the best friend I ever had."

I leaned toward Mark and lowered my voice. "If Uncle Stan really didn't know her name, then Russ wouldn't have gained anything by killing him. All he'd have done was guarantee he'd never become part owner of Sugarwood."

"That's a big *if*," Mark whispered back.

I rubbed the sides of my nose with my fingers where bands of pressure were building. It was a big *if*. And Russ did still have Beaver's Tail beer in his fridge. He still drank it, which meant he had the means to kill Uncle Stan.

"Do you regularly drink Beaver's Tail beer?" I tried to make the question seem like I was circling back around trying to understand the situation better. I didn't play poker, but wasn't there some saying about not showing all your cards?

"I never drink it," Russ said. "I've heard people describe how it tastes and I don't need the caffeine high that bad. My friend brought that one bottle over that night. We were going to drink it together, just to be able to say we'd tried it, but we...got distracted," he finished lamely.

I jumped to counting backward by sevens to try to block out the mental imagery that came with his confession.

If what he said were true, then he wasn't the one who killed Uncle Stan after all. He wouldn't have had a couple cases lying around to use, and odds were good Jason wouldn't have sold him any. Not unless they'd conspired together, which didn't seem likely.

Mark nudged my elbow and mouthed the word *alibi.*

Right. I had to treat this the same way I had Jason regardless. I couldn't assume Russ was innocent simply because I liked him. I knew better. "Where were you the night Uncle Stan died?"

"Here, alone." Russ did this little lift of his whole torso that I interpreted as a shrug. "I could make something up, but then you'd figure out I was lying and be convinced I was guilty."

He might be right. At this point I'd suspect anyone with motive who withheld something.

"You're not going to tell Carl about this, are you?" Russ asked.

Mark would probably say we should tell Chief Wilson, but nothing Russ said directly connected to Uncle Stan's death yet except that we knew why Uncle Stan accused Jason of lying about the strength of his beers. Besides, if the police department turned their attention to Russ, they wouldn't have the manpower to properly investigate Jason, and Jason still seemed like the likelier suspect.

"Not yet." I scooped up the take-out containers and dumped them in the trash. "Like you said, I don't want to cast suspicion on someone who might be innocent."

He met my gaze, his eyes sadder than I'd seen them even at Uncle Stan's funeral. "If Jason killed Stan, I still won't be innocent."

A deep exhaustion settled into my bones. I didn't want Russ to be guilty. I wanted his help and experience running this business. Maybe someday we'd renew the idea of partnering in the business. I wanted the opportunity to build a friendship with the man who'd been Uncle Stan's closest friend for so many years. But now, even if I proved him innocent, he'd likely never be the same.

I needed to check into Jason's alibi myself rather than waiting for Chief Wilson to get around to it. At least then neither Russ nor I would have to wonder anymore.

Chapter 15

I noticed the missed-call message on my cell phone when I came out of the shower the next morning.

Apparently the gas company found the source of my leak. The cause of the leak, however, was indeterminate. That seemed like a nice way of saying *we can't tell if someone tried to blow you up or not.*

Either way, I was cleared to move back in to the house if I wanted to. I didn't. I might be investigating a murder, but that didn't make me one of those too-stupid-to-live sleuths who heard a strange noise in the darkened basement and went to investigate all by herself. I planned to sleep safely at The Sunburnt Arms until we knew who'd killed Uncle Stan or enough time passed that the murderer felt safe and forgot to care about me.

Hopefully it'd be the former so that I wouldn't have to waste a large chunk of the money Uncle Stan left me by staying long-term at a B&B.

I dressed—thankfully I'd found a dry cleaners and been able to use Uncle Stan's washer and dryer prior to the gas incident, so I had fresh clothes again—and climbed into my car.

Since I wasn't planning to move back into Uncle Stan's house right away, I'd need to work on sorting through the rest of the house in the daytime hours.

I was halfway there when my phone rang. I answered through the Bluetooth.

"Is this Nicole?" a male voice asked.

The voice sounded vaguely familiar, but not familiar enough that I could place it. "Yes."

"This is Sergeant Erik Higgins."

Still no bells went off in my head.

"I responded to the gas leak at your house a couple of nights ago."

"Of course. Sorry about not making the connection sooner. I was a bit distracted that night."

"No problem." He had a nice laugh, kind of gravelly and cozy at the same time. "I wanted to make sure someone had called you to let you know you could go home if you wanted...back to your uncle's house I mean, not back to Virginia."

If I'd been in any other town, I'd have wondered how he knew I was from Virginia. Around here, though, I would have been more surprised if he didn't know at least that much about me. "I got a call this morning, but I appreciate you checking in."

The spaces between houses stretched out as I reached the edge of town. Uncle Stan's driveway was the last one before fields and forests completely took over the landscape. A sign at the road directed drivers as to which fork in the driveway to take for tours and shopping, and I'd become comfortable enough with the other branches now to know without thinking which forks also led to Uncle Stan's house, as well as Russ' and Noah's places. They were the only two staff to live on site, their accommodations one of the perks that came with their positions.

Sergeant Higgins hadn't disconnected the call by the time I reached the driveway. "Was there something else you needed, Sergeant?"

"Erik." He cleared his throat. "Call me Erik."

Ooohhhh. I got it now. This wasn't really an official call at all.

"I was wondering if you might be free for drinks on Friday night," he said.

It was official—my dating prospects were apparently going to be better here than they had been back home. I wasn't going to get too high on myself, though. It was more likely because I was fresh blood than because I was anything special.

Still, I couldn't think of any reason not to go. He'd seemed nice enough, and going out with a friendly police officer was a much better option than sitting at home and wishing Mark wasn't married.

I parked in the driveway of Uncle Stan's house. "Sure. What time?"

We arranged a few details like whether we'd meet at whatever spot we decided on or if he'd pick me up.

"Anyplace you'd like to try?" Erik asked.

I drummed my fingers on the steering wheel. Would it be duplicitous or merely efficient to suggest Hops, where I could also try to sneak some information from the bartender about the validity of Jason's alibi? It's not like I'd spend the whole night investigating. And it would solve the internal debate I'd been having with myself about asking Mark to go with me to Hops, which would have felt much too much like a date.

I would have flipped a coin if I had one, but in lieu of that, I'd toss the decision into his court. "I don't know many places, but I heard of one called Hops. Is it any good?"

"On Fridays and Saturdays it is. They open the kitchen even in the off-season. It's only greasy bar fare, fried onion blossoms and sliders and stuff like that, but it's the best heart-attack-on-a-plate food around. We could go early and grab dinner, too, if you'd like."

Why not? Since I didn't actually drink, I'd always preferred an actual meal to going out for drinks. My friends back home said that was too much of a commitment for a first date. What if the guy turned out to be a dud? I'd personally never understood how they could decide with only a few drinks if they wanted to see someone again or not. I liked the extra time that came with dinner, and how clear could your judgment be about a guy after a couple of drinks anyway?

We agreed to meet at 6:00 on Friday night. In the meantime, I'd plan my approach to discreetly checking Jason's alibi and make sure nothing else turned up in Uncle Stan's papers to shift my search in another direction.

The next night I picked the jeans that made my bi-cycler's thighs look thinner and my favorite royal blue blouse that made my eyes extra blue. Not that Erik hadn't already seen me with bed head wrapped in a blanket. He scored points for asking me out after seeing me look like that.

Erik must not have been kidding when he said it was some of the best food around because I almost couldn't find a spot when I pulled into the parking lot.

I burst through the door to Hops at exactly 6:00. And that was not how I'd been raised. *Show up early to everything because it's disrespectful to keep people waiting* was the mantra in my house growing up.

I ground to a halt as soon as I was inside. I'd only seen Erik in the weird glow of police cruiser lights and the dim interior of the car itself. If you'd asked me to pick him out of a lineup, I probably couldn't do it. And the bar was so full that a lineup would have given me fewer options.

Just as my stomach was starting to turn, a man stood up from a table near the back and waved at me. The broad shoulders were a giveaway even if the wave hadn't been. He wasn't heavy-set by any means, but I might have called him husky. He was built like a line-backer, a wall of solid muscle, and his hair, which I was seeing for the first time, was buzzed military short. He'd picked the chair at the table that allowed him to have his back to the wall and a clear view of the rest of the room.

I'd keep it in mind to ask him if he was former military if there was a lull in the conversation. Social rule #1 on my mother's list: Always have a topic in mind to keep a conversation going. Maybe that's why I was chronically uncomfortable with any silence longer than ten seconds. Yeah, that's the story I was going with rather than that it was a flaw in my DNA.

My preparations weren't necessary. After the initial awkward I'm-no-longer-a-victim-you're-interviewing-for-work moments, we settled into an easy conversation. It was different than talking to Mark, less goofiness, more deep discussion, but still nice. Very nice. Almost too nice, since the evening was nearly over before I remembered why I'd suggested Hops in the first place.

"I'll be right back," I said, motioning in the general direction of the restrooms, which also happened to be the direction of the bar.

I wouldn't have much time to come at this subtly. Then again, I was in a bar. Subtle wasn't exactly the word of the hour.

I waited for the crowd ordering drinks to part for a minute and I hopped up on a stool.

The bartender stopped in front of me. "What'll it be?"

"Are you Kevin Franklin?"

His eyes narrowed slightly. "Yeah."

I held out a $20. Hopefully money talked here. "I was hoping you could help me with something. Was Jason Wood in here a week ago last Saturday night, negotiating with you to carry his beers?"

Whatever reason he thought I had for asking, he snagged my $20. "Not on a Saturday, that's for sure. You see this place." He swept a hand toward the room behind me. "You think I'd have time to argue with Jason on a night like this."

Busted. It still didn't prove Jason killed Uncle Stan, but it did prove he wasn't where he said he was the night Uncle Stan died.

I smiled at Kevin and slid down from the stool. "Thanks."

I turned around and came face to chest with Erik.

A little frown left creases between his eyes. "I came to make sure you weren't buying your own drink. Why do you care where Jason Wood was?"

Crap. Asking about another guy did not look good on a first date. And it'd be nice to have a second. He was a gentleman. We had a surprising amount in common. And, most importantly, he wasn't married. At least not that I knew of. He didn't have a wedding ring on or a mark on his ring finger where one might have been.

I tipped my chin up toward our table. We settled in and he leaned back with his arms crossed over his chest. Not a good sign.

"I've been looking into my uncle's murder, which is why someone might have tried to blow me up the other night and why I was asking where Jason was the night my uncle died, because I think he might have been the one who killed him." It all came out in a sonic speed information dump.

Erik blinked slowly, but his arms loosened from his chest. "Is that why you wanted to try Hops tonight?"

Burning started in my ears and spread across my cheeks. I dropped my gaze. "Yes."

"Is that the only reason you agreed to go out with me tonight?"

I swear I was doomed to be single forever. "No. But when you asked if there was anywhere I wanted to go, this was the place that came to mind."

"And is there a reason you didn't tell me?"

I brought my gaze up. He was giving me the same granite stare I imagined he used on suspects he was questioning. I couldn't read it. That wasn't a feeling I was comfortable with.

"I knew how it would look." I pursed my lips. If I was being honest, I might as well confess to all of it. "And Chief Wilson technically told me to stop investigating."

His lips twitched. I couldn't quite tell if it was amusement or a simple muscle spasm. "I *have* heard that you've been a stone in his boot."

I tucked my hair behind my ears. "I understand if you want to call it a night."

His stare didn't change. "I do." He pushed back his seat and stood.

Way to go, Nik. I slumped slightly in my seat.

His hand clamped on the chair back and helped pull it out for me. "But I think you owe me another date to make up for it."

I glanced up at him. His lips twitched again. It must be his version of a smile. "I can do that."

He walked with me to the bar door. People seemed to naturally part in front of him, unlike the way I'd had to squeeze through the tightly packed bodies and say *excuse me* at least five times in my attempt to reach the bar.

He held open the door, and I ducked outside. The cold air slapped me in the face, and I sucked in a breath. With all the bodies packed into Hops, it'd been so warm I'd forgotten how far north I was.

I hitched a thumb to the right. "I'm that way."

"I'm in the other direction." He reached for my hand and linked his fingers with mine. "I'll call you later this week. Next time, though, tell me what you're up to. I could have questioned Kevin officially."

I gently squeezed his hand. "I will. Promise." I gave him a lopsided smile. "Are you going to tell Chief Wilson?"

"I should tell him that Jason's alibi fell through, don't you think?"

I picked at one of my buttons with my free hand. "Do you have to tell him I'm the one who checked it?"

He gave the hand he held a return squeeze, then let go. "Yup. Omission is still a lie."

I wobbled a little like his words came with a physical push. It was such a different perspective from what I'd been raised with. My parents were masters of omission. They considered it good business practice. I guess in their work—our work—it was. Maybe the Chihuahua-size lump his words created in my stomach were yet another sign that I wasn't cut out to continue working as a defense attorney. Lying—directly or by omission—tended to make me feel like a sleaze.

"I'll give him a call right away so he doesn't waste time sending anyone else out here." He raised his hand in a parting wave. "Goodnight, Nicole. Try to stay safe. I plan to make good on calling in that second date."

I blushed again, but this time for an entirely different reason.

Chapter 16

Since I wasn't going to be able to sleep anytime soon with my mind bouncing from my date with Erik to Jason's broken alibi, I headed for Sugarwood instead of for The Sunburnt Arms. No way was I staying out there after dark, but I could quickly grab the last two boxes and haul them back to my room at the B&B to sort through. I still hadn't found the insurance papers, and I was guessing I only had a limited amount of time to get those changed over into my name before the policy would lapse.

I pulled up in front of Uncle Stan's house. I needed to start thinking of it as my house, but that was going to take me a while longer. Once I settled in and didn't have to worry about someone trying to blow me up again, I could redecorate and put my own touch on the place. Then, hopefully, it would start to feel more like home.

I fished around under my passenger seat and snagged the flashlight I'd bought myself earlier today. I popped it on, and immediately my heart rate slowed. It was startling the difference a little extra light could make. I made my way up the walk.

A piece of paper tacked to the front door fluttered gently in the breeze. I freed it. The paper was smooth, a sure sign it hadn't been there long, not with all the random showers we'd had today.

I aimed the flashlight beam at the paper.

Nicole,

There's a dangerous mold problem with the old sugar shack that could hurt business. I need your help with a decision immediately. Please meet me there as soon as you get in.

--Russ

I glanced over my shoulder toward the path that led to the original sugar shack. I couldn't see further than a few feet away unless my flashlight were aimed in that direction.

A shiver slithered over my arms. Russ made it sound urgent. I honestly didn't know enough about this business yet to know if that was melodrama or if snap decisions were often needed.

Mold could make people quite sick depending on the kind. How long did it take to cure mold? The tours given of the grounds made up a significant portion of income during the busy season, especially for Noah, who'd told me about the generous tips people gave him if he let their kids feed the horses carrots, and the original sugar shack was one of the popular highlights.

I squinted into the dark. I tucked the flashlight under my arm and worked my phone out of my purse. I'd give him a call first.

My phone showed one weak bar of signal. Great. First thing tomorrow morning, I was calling local carriers and seeing if one could give me the best coverage, penalty or no penalty for canceling my current contract before it ended.

I'd gotten a signal inside the house before. I unlocked the door. I wasn't traipsing out there in the dark until I'd exhausted my other options.

Inside, my signal jumped to full. I dialed Russ. No answer. The old sugar shack probably sat in another pocket.

I chewed on my bottom lip. Stay or go. He might not even be out there anymore.

Or he might be waiting for a chance to ambush you, the paranoid voice in my head said.

"Shut up," I told it.

I knew I could outrun Russ as long as he didn't get a firm hold on me. I might be too clumsy for sports, but I loved running and biking. The only way I'd be in danger was if he had a gun, and that wouldn't look much like an accident.

Besides, Jason didn't have an alibi. Russ looked less and less like a suspect every second.

Just in case, I ducked into the kitchen and grabbed a steak knife. I hid it in my purse. None of my self-defense training included knives, but how hard could it be? Stab for your attacker's fleshy parts, then run. It'd only be a backup anyway.

I quickly moved the last boxes I needed to sort through into my car, locked the house and car, and headed into the woods with my flashlight.

On second thought...I backtracked and unlocked my car. In case I needed a quick getaway, I didn't want to be struggling to find my keys and unlock my car while running.

I shook my head. "Now you're being silly. And you're talking to yourself."

But I'd rather be silly than dead. And no one was around to see my silly, so it didn't matter. If I didn't need the knife or the unlocked car, no one would be the wiser, and they both made me feel a whole lot better about heading off into the woods alone.

I passed into the tree line and held the flashlight out in front of me like a shield. It wouldn't stave off a human attacker, but hopefully it would keep the creepy crawlies in the woods away from me. Did they have wolves up here?

I strode forward, my speed a touch shy of a jog. I wasn't cut out for the great outdoors.

Cold stiffened my fingers. The old sugar shack appeared in front of me, all shadows and reflection. A light glowed from inside.

"Russ?"

No answer.

I moved around the front. The door was hooked open and a fire burned under the boiler. He must have been waiting for me and stepped away to take care of something else.

I climbed inside and directed my flashlight beam into the corners and around the edges of the floorboards. No mold that I could see.

A grinding sound behind me. I whirled around in time to see the front door slam close with a shack-rattling bang.

I dove for the door and tugged on the handle. It refused to budge.

My heart skittered around in my chest and the jittery feeling spiraled through my stomach and head. I swallowed hard. *Do not panic.*

Russ told me the door sometimes did this. The hook must not have been properly set. Maybe I'd jostled it when I climbed in.

I whipped my phone out to call for help. No signal.

I sank down into the chair, gulping in air. It was a simple accident. This wasn't a big deal. Russ would come back and let me out. No one stood to gain anything from locking me in here. Even if, for some strange reason, Russ didn't come back to check for me

or put out the fire, I wouldn't freeze to death overnight. I had a fire, after all. Noah would be by to feed
the horses in the barn tomorrow morning, and he'd
have to hear me if I yelled. If nothing else, Mark would
start to worry if he didn't hear from me in a few days.
My mom or Fay or Erik might even start to wonder
what happened to me. I could live a few days without
food and water.

I hugged my purse and flashlight into my lap.
"Don't be a baby, Nicole."

Nicole!

The note taped to my door hadn't called me Nikki.
It'd called me Nicole. But Russ, at least in verbal com-
munication, always called me Nikki. What if Russ
hadn't left the note at all?

I pulled it out of my pocket and read it again. Anyone could have written it. I didn't know Russ's handwriting, and it didn't have anything in it that had to
come from Russ.

And I'd fallen for it.

But if Russ hadn't sent it, why had whoever did
want to draw me here?

A sharp crack ripped through the air, like wood
snapping. I jumped to my feet, my purse, flashlight,
and the note tumbling to the ground. What the...?

I inched toward the back of the building. Heat radi-
ated off the wall. I stretched out my hand, but yanked
it back before touching the wood.

Holy. Crap. They'd set the building on fire from the outside.

I backed toward my chair in the middle of the room. My hands shook, and I couldn't steady them. The fire under the boiler made sense now. Depending on if they'd used an accelerant, or if the police even brought in an arson investigator to check for accelerants, this could very well look like an accident. Stupid city girl was fooling around with the equipment in the old sugar shack and burned it down with herself inside.

It was a flimsy cover. They had to be depending on law enforcement to not investigate too carefully. After nearly getting away with Uncle Stan's murder, they had good reason to think that might be the case. Except I didn't think Mark would believe this was an accident.

For all the good that would do me. I'd be dead.

I checked my phone. Still no signal. No way to call for help. By the time someone noticed the flames, it'd be too late. I had to find a way out myself.

Smoke poured in the cracks, and a bead of sweat trickled down the back of my neck under my hair. I stripped off my jacket.

There were only two ways out of the shack. The door, which I knew was locked tightly, perhaps even secured from the outside to make sure I didn't escape. And a tiny window high in the left wall.

I dragged the chair across to the window and stepped up. The fire must have been set on the opposite side, on the wall behind the boiler, because this wall was still cool. The window was clean, and I couldn't see any flames directly outside it either.

The window was small, but assuming I could get it open, I should be able to climb out. And once I got out, I'd have to hope I didn't break my neck in the fall.

I ran my fingers along the edges of the window. It wasn't the kind that opened, and it had a sturdy wooden bar running horizontal across the middle and another vertical. Breaking out the glass would be easy enough. The bars would be the real problem.

I scrambled down from the chair, grabbed my jacket, and wrapped it around my hand and arm. I snagged one of the antique-looking spiky metal tools from its hanger on the wall and smashed out the glass as well as I could. None of the other tools looked like they'd help me with the bars.

Smoke dried out my throat, and I scrubbed at my eyes. Sweat plastered my hair to the back of my neck.

I wrenched on the bars. Even if I hung off of them, they didn't feel like they'd give. I had to weaken them somehow.

A cough wracked my body. The air even seemed hot now as I breathed it in. I was too afraid to look back. A panic attack now would, quite literally, kill me.

I grabbed my purse. The only thing I could think was to saw at the bars with the steak knife I'd wedged into my purse. It was the heavy kind that men seemed to favor, and if I knew my uncle, it would be sharp.

I took out the knife and heaved my purse out the window. Assuming I didn't make it, maybe someone would spot my purse and see it as a clue that this was no accident.

My lungs burned and ached. I sawed at the vertical bar with both hands wrapped around the knife handle. Even without looking, I could tell by the roaring and firecracker-like pops behind me that I wouldn't have time to cut through both. If I could at least break this one off, I *might* be able to squeeze through. I wasn't chunky, but I wouldn't be modeling on any runways, either. I carried a lot of muscle weight.

The wooden bar started to splinter. I yanked on it, leaning back, and the bar gave at the bottom. I shoved it back and forth until the top broke. I dropped it on the floor inside. One less thing to fall on if I could get out.

I stuck my arm out the window and heaved the knife to the side, out of my drop radius hopefully but where I could still grab it back up in case the arsonist decided to stick around to watch me burn. What kind of a psycho would do that, knowing he'd probably hear my dying screams, I don't know, but I wasn't taking any chances.

I hoisted myself up and shoved my upper half through the window. Shards of glass I couldn't remove tore my shirt and sliced my skin, sending lines of pain down my torso. Each squirm delivered new streaks of hot pain. The horizontal wooden bar ground into my back.

One final twist and I tumbled out the window, trying desperately to push off the wall and shift my weight so I wouldn't fall on my head.

I hit the ground sideways. Something popped in my shoulder, and agony burst through my body. Black rimmed my vision, and the hot, queasy feeling that always came before passing out flooded over me.

But I was still too close. I used the building wall to pull myself up, but my vision blacked completely and I sank to the ground. I crawled as far as I could from the shack using my good arm. My other arm dangled in a strange way. I tried not to think about it.

Somewhere between the shack and the edge of the clearing, I passed out.

Chapter 17

When I next remembered opening my eyes, I was in a room with tan walls. My shoulder still ached, and I felt the sling before I focused enough to see it. I ran my good hand over my torso. Someone had bandaged me up.

Soft male voices started to register. Ones I recognized. Mark? And Russ?

My stomach knotted. The use of my full first name wasn't solid proof that he hadn't sent that note. Maybe he was the kind of person who would always write my full name even though he called me Nikki.

And whoever wanted to get rid of me had almost succeeded a second time. I wasn't going to test the old saying that the third time's a charm. After I figured out whether I was seriously injured, I needed to talk to Mark alone.

I turned my head. Russ and Mark stood outside what I now realized was my hospital room. Someone must have spotted the fire or found me.

"Hey." Russ pointed toward me. "She's awake."

They strode into my room, and Russ moved to my bedside and laid a hand on my shoulder.

I recoiled, my body reacting instinctively even though my mind was unconvinced Russ could have done this to me.

Russ jerked his hand back. "Sorry. You're probably sore, aren't you?"

"How did I get here?" I asked. My voice came out raspy, and it hurt my throat to speak.

"Noah saw flames when he was coming home last night." Russ scrubbed his hands over the top of his head. "He called 9-1-1 right away and went straight to the spot. He found the sugar shack burning and you passed out about forty feet away. That's when he called me and I called Mark." He wrung his hands together. "I thought you might want him here."

I struggled to sit up. Mark helped me. The blanket slumped down, revealing a blue hospital gown. I wasn't going to ask where my clothes were. They probably hadn't been salvageable. "Am I okay?"

Mark sank down into the chair next to my bed. "Other than a dislocated shoulder, your wounds were relatively minor cuts and bruises. The doctors wouldn't tell us anything at first, so I used your cell phone to call your mom and had her give them permission to share your medical information with me since she couldn't be here."

I scrunched my eyes shut. Perfect. Now my mom would think staying was an even worse idea, and she'd also think Mark and I were involved. The idea of her daughter dating a doctor might almost make up for the fact that I nearly died. "You talked to my mom."

"I hope that's okay." His voice carried a hesitant note. "I waited until after the hospital notified her, of course."

I forced open my eyes and smiled at him. Thinking logically, he'd done the right thing. I'd clean up the Mom mess later. "No, that's fine." I pulled the blanket up a little higher. The thin sheet and even thinner hospital gown weren't nearly warm enough, and it felt like my bra had gone wherever the rest of my clothes had. "Did they say when I could leave?"

"Assuming your neurological scans come back clean, later today."

I felt my head. "I don't think I hit my head when I fell."

Mark flashed me his dimples. "They have to check. You were unconscious when Noah found you, and we had no idea what happened."

The unspoken question of what had happened hung in the air. I flickered a glance toward Russ. "Could you go call Chief Wilson for me, please? I assume he'll want to take my statement." That might not take him long enough for what I needed to do. "And would you try to find me a cup of coffee? I could really use something warm to drink."

A relieved look flashed across Russ's face. I got the feeling from the stretched-thin look around his eyes and the way he held stiff like he was afraid to touch anything that he didn't like hospitals. He'd come here, to a place that made him uncomfortable, for my sake. That either made him especially caring or especially smart, since playing the role of concerned friend would help him seem innocent.

"'Course," he said. "I'll find you a snack too."

He waddled out of the room, squeezing hand sanitizer into his palms from a tiny bottle he'd pulled from his pocket. I wouldn't have pegged him for a germaphobe.

I twisted the hospital blanket into a clump in my fist. What else didn't I know about him? Maybe he had done this.

Mark's hand rested on my bed railing, and I longed for the comfort of human touch. For a second I found myself actually wishing my mom or dad had been worried enough about me to come up, even though I knew they wouldn't actually have made it here by now. I wanted to curl into someone's arms and be hugged for a few minutes and feel safe.

Because I clearly wasn't safe here.

If we didn't find who did this, I might never be safe here.

"I can't stay here unless we figure out who did this," I blurted out.

Mark took my hand and wrapped it in his. He rubbed his thumb along my knuckles. "Slow down. Start from the beginning and tell me what happened."

I recapped everything for him, including the note.

He gave a slow nod of his head. "That's why you sent Russ away."

Tears built behind my eyes. In my mind I heard my mom's voice lecturing me about image and strength, especially in a female lawyer. I swallowed the tears down even though no one other than my mom could really blame me for wanting to cry when I'd narrowly escaped being roasted alive. "I don't want to believe he did this, he's been so kind to me, but his name was on the note."

"You also said he addressed it to Nicole, not to Nikki."

I nodded. "But I can't take the chance. Right? I shouldn't take the chance."

I wanted to pinch myself to make me shut up. I knew I was sounding a touch hysterical. The first time could have been an accidental gas leak. This time had to be intentional. No one had ever tried to kill me before, and I wasn't exactly a brave person. I was the opposite of brave. Now that I was safe for the moment, all the mental resolve I'd had earlier crumbled around me.

His thumb kept stroking in soothing motions. "You shouldn't take the chance. We'll have to tell Carl about the note, but I think he'll also want to find out if Jason had an alibi for last night."

"Does Russ have an alibi for last night?"

Mark's shoulders drooped. "He was alone when Noah called him."

Four hours later, I signed my release forms. I'd sent Russ back to Sugarwood to deal with clean-up and to assess what we'd need to rebuild a replica shack, and I'd given my statement to Chief Wilson, who promised to check Jason's alibi for last night before the end of the day.

I didn't believe he actually would until my phone rang while I limped down the hall after Mark, wearing a pair of yoga pants and a t-shirt he'd brought for me. They weren't mine, and I'd had to roll the pant legs up to keep from tripping on them. I didn't know where he'd gotten them from. I didn't ask. If I was wearing his wife's clothes, I didn't want to know.

The caller ID identified the police station, and I nearly dropped my phone in my haste to answer it.

"Are you alright?"

The phone slipped again, and I gripped it tighter. The voice on the other end wasn't Chief Wilson. It was Erik.

"I just heard about the attack," he said.

Mark waved at me from a few feet away and mouthed the words *you okay?* I held back a fidget and nodded. It was more than a little uncomfortable talking to Erik while standing with Mark.

"I will be." The words served to answer both men's question about my well-being. "I scratched myself up escaping from the sugar shack and then dislocated my shoulder in the fall. But nothing that won't heal."

Mark made a walking motion with his fingers and then mimed driving. I bit my bottom lip a touch and smiled. He was such a goof for a medical examiner. I nodded to let him know he could bring the car around front and I'd meet him there.

Erik cleared his throat in the way that I was beginning to recognize signaled nervousness. "Listen, I have some bad news for you. About the suspected arsonist."

My stomach dropped. Did he mean Russ or Jason? I prayed to Uncle Stan's God that he wasn't about to tell me they had evidence that Russ was the one who tried to kill me.

"We went out to Beaver's Tail Brewery today to check into Jason Wood's alibi for last night."

"Oh," I said.

It was all I could force out past the relief. This had nothing to do with Russ. If the bad news was about Jason, I didn't care what it was.

"As we drove up," Erik said, "I spotted him sneaking off into the woods behind his place, so we followed him. We caught him working an illegal still with two other guys. From the look of their setup, they were trying to find a way to distill marijuana into beer."

"That sounds like good news." But that nervous, regretful tone was still in his voice. I was missing something. "What's the bad news?"

"The men he was with alibied him for both last night and the night Stan died."

I sank into a nearby chair. With Jason alibied out, that meant... "Could they be lying?"

"That's always a possibility." He blew out a breath. "But that's not my read on it. They admitted to everything else in exchange for a deal. They'd have no reason to give Jason an alibi for Stan's murder or for attempting to murder you. I'm sorry. I think the guy who attacked you is still out there."

I hunched over, my good elbow propped on my knee, phone still to my ear. He didn't understand the real blow. If it wasn't Jason, it had to be Russ.

Chapter 18

I stumbled zombie-like out to Mark's truck, or at least I was expecting to see Mark's truck. Instead I saw my car. It was such a small thing...but it was a huge thing. To not have to climb into his truck when I was hurting.

I slid in and ran my hands lovingly over the upholstery.

"Russ thought you'd be more comfortable in your own car," Mark said.

Russ thought. I thumped my head back against the headrest. More than once.

Mark shot me a look that said he wasn't sure whether he should drive or take me back in for a psych eval.

I kept my head back and my eyes closed. "Jason has an alibi. He's not the one who locked me in last night."

Mark didn't say anything in response. He put the car into drive and pulled away from the hospital.

I didn't know how much time had passed before I realized he was driving us in circles.

"Are you figuring out how to apologize again?" I asked, trying to lighten the mood.

He gave me a half-smile, but it died before it could fully form. "I've known Russ my whole life. He was engaged to my aunt before she died of cancer. I've never even heard him raise his voice, let alone... I just don't..." He shook his head.

I didn't get it either. "The question I still can't answer is *why*. Why kill my uncle? If Russ isn't naturally a killer, isn't naturally violent, then it should have taken a much bigger trigger to push him into killing his best friend, shouldn't it?"

Mark shrugged. "I would have thought so."

Or perhaps we were both blinded by the kind of man we wanted to see Russ as. If I only knew why, maybe I could accept it better. Sure, some people killed for the pleasure or challenge of it. Most people needed a more concrete motive.

A thought that had been swimming around in my subconscious finally made its way to the surface. Tom McClanahan said Uncle Stan changed his will about a month ago. Who had been set to inherit Sugarwood before he left it to me? Now that I'd seen how much love he'd poured into the place and its employees, I had a hard time believing he would have left it to my father, who disdained every aspect of Uncle Stan's life here. "What time is it?"

"Just before five. Why?"

"I need to go to Tom McClanahan's office."

Mark gave me another glance hinting he wanted a closer look at my head, but he pulled a U-turn anyway. "Are you going to tell me what we're doing when we get there?"

I didn't want to talk about it, but I owed him that much at least. He'd sat with me in the hospital all day, and now he was driving me wherever I asked him to. "I have an idea about what Russ' real motive might have been, but I won't know for sure until we get there."

He parked out front and tried the door. It was locked.

I checked my watch. 5:01 pm. I pressed my face close to the glass. Ashley sat at her desk inside. Hopefully that meant Tom McClanahan was still here as well.

I pounded on the door, making the glass rattle.

I could almost hear Ashley's condescending sigh. She crossed the room and cracked the door.

"We're closed," she said in a tone that suggested I must be stupid for not understanding the locked door.

Her gaze ran over my clothes in that way some women have of implying they'd never be caught in public looking like you. I swear her lip actually curled a little.

Normally a look like that would have withered me, just one more reminder of how I failed to live up to my potential and to what was expected of me. This time it made me sad for her instead. Maybe the soot still clinging to my hair, the sling on my arm, and the too-large clothes had a shielding effect. Or maybe almost dying did have a way of putting things into perspective the way people said it did.

Mark pressed in beside me. "Is Tom still in? We just need a minute."

She drew her shoulders back, making her cleavage almost impossible to miss. To his credit, Mark didn't even sneak a peek.

Ashley opened the door wider. "Why don't you come in and I'll check for you?"

The smile she flashed him belonged in a dental ad, too wide and all teeth and fake as her veneers.

The urge to lie and tell her she had lipstick on her teeth was almost more than I could stand. But that would have been mean. And petty. And while I could have met her attitude with snark of my own, that wasn't the kind of person I wanted to be. Bad enough I had a tendency to lie and manipulate.

I lowered my achy body into one of the waiting room chairs. I'd barely made it down when Ashley emerged from Tom McClanahan's office, followed by the man himself.

He shook hands with Mark. "Is there an emergency?"

Mark stepped aside to reveal me slumped in the chair that was cushy enough I was considering a nap. "I'm here as support only. Nicole's actually the one who needs to speak with you."

Tom McClanahan pushed his wire-rimmed glasses a little higher up his face. "Why don't you both follow me."

If it hadn't been for Ashley, I might have talked to him in the waiting room so I didn't have to leave the chair. As it was, I hoisted myself up and we trailed him into his office like obedient puppies.

This time he didn't take a perch on the corner of his desk. He moved straight to his chair, sat, and steepled his fingers. "I admit, you have me curious."

I already felt like the life force was draining out of me and slopping all over his carpets. The sooner I could return to my bed at The Sunburnt Arms, the better. No subtlety this time. "I'm going to assume that you were my Uncle Stan's lawyer for as long as he lived in Fair Haven. Last time I was in here, you told me he recently changed his will. Do you have a copy of the previous version?"

McClanahan shook his head. "I'm afraid not. Previous versions of the will aren't valid, so we dispose of them."

Okay, so we wouldn't have the solid evidence I hoped for, but McClanahan was a respected member of the community, and his testimony would still be weighed heavily if it came to that. "Do you remember who he left Sugarwood to prior to bequeathing everything to me?"

"Of course," he said. "I have an excellent memory for each of my clients, despite their number. He'd originally left Sugarwood to Russell Dantry."

Crap. Crap crap crap crap crap. Expecting it didn't make hearing it any better.

Mark buried his face in his hands.

Tom McClanahan leaned back in his seat, a bemused expression on his face. "I gather that's not what you wanted to hear."

I shook my head and rose to my feet. "Unfortunately not. But thank you for taking the time to see me after hours."

I brushed my fingers across Mark's shoulder. He raised his head. His face was drawn.

I'm sorry, I mouthed.

He nodded and we left the office together.

When we got back into the car, we sat there without talking for at least ten minutes. When Uncle Stan refused to move forward with the partnership, Russ must have felt he had only one option to get Sugarwood for himself. Sometime in their partnership discussions, it must have come up that Russ was already in Uncle Stan's will to inherit the place upon his death. What Uncle Stan must have neglected to tell Russ was that he switched it to me. He'd probably been waiting for the right time, since they weren't regularly speaking and he hadn't even had a chance to tell me yet.

I couldn't tell what Mark was thinking based on his expression, but I swung from denial to anger to an irrational sense that I was betraying Russ by taking this information to the powers that be. Which was stupid. He'd tried to kill me. It had to have been him. He loved Sugarwood.

What must it be like to know so strongly what you wanted from your life? I'd never want to kill someone to have my desire fulfilled, but I'd like to at least feel that certainty of *what* I wanted.

"I have to tell Chief Wilson." My voice sounded strange, all small and hollow, in the abnormally silent interior of the car.

"I know," Mark said.

He turned on the car and drove. Without him saying anything, I knew he was headed for the police department.

Mark slammed a fist on the steering wheel and let out a low curse. I jumped.

"Sorry." He glanced my way. "I'm not excusing what he did, but Sugarwood was his whole life. Something inside him must have snapped when he thought he might lose it."

It was my turn to say, "I know."

Chief Wilson clearly knew as well. When we marched into his office and told him everything, from the note to what we'd learned, he sent men to arrest Russ for the murder of Uncle Stan.

Chapter 19

I'd expected solving Uncle Stan's murder to feel good—like a Batman-esque, paragon-of-justice, euphoric high. Maybe I should have known better. Batman never seemed particularly happy in any of the movies I'd seen.

And I hadn't counted on the killer being a man I'd grown to like.

Once Mark dropped me off and disappeared on foot down the street, I found myself limping to the convenience store on the corner and buying one of every variety of candy bar they carried. Even the ones with nuts that I hated. A giant slushie and a package of gummy bears may have also been involved.

I holed up in The Sunburnt Arms, not even answering my phone for the next few days, though I did send my mom a text to let her know I was alive.

In lieu of a response asking how I was feeling, she wrote back *So is there something I should know about this doctor friend of yours?*

He's married, I texted.

I didn't feel her reply of *Happily?* merited a return text.

Happily or unhappily didn't matter. Fool me once, shame on you. Fool me twice, and I'd deserve whatever I got. I might have eaten my way through enough chocolate to make me look like an acne-ridden teenager again, but I wasn't completely driven by my hormones.

By the third night, I was out of the microwave dinners, bag of apples, and bottled water I'd stocked my mini-fridge with when I moved in post-gas leak. It was time to emerge back into the world. Especially since it was also time to make a decision about whether I stayed in Fair Haven or went home. I couldn't hide out in The Sunburnt Arms forever.

If I went home, my parents would happily take me back into the firm and revive their hope that I was simply a late bloomer and I'd become a decent lawyer with age and continued instruction. Love—and I did believe they loved me or they wouldn't have tried so hard—made them blind to the truth. I'd never be more than mediocre.

My phone rang as I was on my way down the stairs. Erik.

He'd called once a day since Russ was arrested. He only left a voice mail the first time. I needed to answer before he thought I was brushing him off.

When I answered, he didn't ask why I'd ignored his calls. He didn't mention the missed calls at all. He simply asked how I was.

And I had no idea how to answer. "Hungry," I said stupidly.

"I was going to get around to asking if you'd like to have dinner again soon, but I don't think that'll help with your current hunger pains."

I might not still be here in a few days, and he deserved to hear that in person. I owed him that much at least for basically turning our first date into an investigation. "Are you busy now?"

The happiness in his voice as we arranged to meet at A Salt & Battery made me feel like someone had poked me in the heart. Instead of driving there, I walked. I needed to start burning off the chocolate binge.

He was waiting when I came in, once again at a table where he could keep the wall to his back and his face to the room. He got to his feet and pulled out my chair for me. Like I was special.

He handed me a gift bag. I held it in my hands, unopened, for an awkwardly long time. It wouldn't be fair to keep whatever it was if I left, and based on what I'd seen of Erik so far, I was going to want to keep it.

He shifted in his seat and cleared his throat. "It's a get well gift. I thought about flowers, but this seemed more practical."

I peeled back the yellow and pink tissue paper. Inside lay a pale blue scarf and matching set of mittens. They were so soft they could have been made of clouds. I was right. I should have handed it back unopened.

"Do you like them?" he asked.

It was such a surreal situation to be facing a strong man who could somehow also seem so vulnerable. In my experience, those two rarely went together.

"I do." I pushed the bag across the table toward him. "But I can't accept them."

He nudged them back in my direction. "I knew you might think it was too fast for gifts or something, but I noticed you didn't have a set when we went out, and you'll need them for the winters here."

If I had bangs, I would have shot a puff of air at them. I was terrible when it came to men. Everything I tried ended up knotted and bungled. "It's not that at all. But I might not stay in Fair Haven."

The waiter came before Erik could answer and took our orders. I decided to try the perch since the menu said it was a local specialty.

"What changed your mind?" he asked when we were alone again.

It was such a straightforward question. It caught me off guard. And made me want to tell him the truth. That was probably one of his interrogation skills, but I didn't care. "Russ."

He didn't probe, just sat there waiting for me to continue when I was ready. Whether through training or natural ability, the man was an excellent listener.

"I was going to stay because I didn't want to be a lawyer anymore," I said. "I didn't want to defend people who were guilty. It didn't feel right."

"But it doesn't feel right when you have to bring evidence against someone you wanted to be innocent, either."

I nodded. I'd been here before, in this situation, where guilt and innocence didn't seem to fall in the places they should. Erik was one person who could understand that. As a police officer, he'd probably had to arrest people who he'd rather have set free. "I guess I thought I could escape it here. Like the lines of good and evil would be cleaner here in a small town compared to a city, and I'd be able to tell by looking at them who I could trust."

He stretched his hand across the table toward me, palm up. I slid my hand into his.

He wrapped his fingers around mine. "I don't think that's true anywhere. Was that the only reason you thought you'd stay?"

"Originally maybe, but I like it here. I like being able to walk to places, and I kind of even like people knowing me and wanting to know about my life. In the city, I felt faceless, like I could disappear and most people wouldn't even notice. I didn't realize that bothered me until I came here."

His lips twitched in his this-is-as-close-as-I-get-to-a-smile way. "That's certainly not true here."

We ate the rest of our meal without coming back to the topic of Russ or of whether I'd stay or go. I got the sense that Erik didn't want to pressure me. I had to want to stay here for me, not for what might or might not happen between us.

I don't know that I'd ever had someone care so much about what I wanted before.

He drove me back to The Sunburnt Arms after dinner and walked me to the front door. He didn't try to kiss me. Instead he pressed the bag holding the scarf and mitts into my hands.

"Just in case," he said. "If you're not sure what you want from life yet, this isn't a bad place to find out. It's how I ended up here."

And then he was gone.

Chapter 20

Early the next morning I packed everything into my car and checked out of The Sunburnt Arms. It was time to go home. I felt a little like a kid who'd figured out that the Easter bunny wasn't real, which meant that by extension Santa Claus and the Tooth Fairy didn't exist, either.

Fair Haven wasn't the enchanted place I'd built it up in my mind to be from Uncle Stan's praise of it. People here still lied and cheated as much as in DC. And I was no Matlock. I might as well go back to defending people I knew were guilty. At least then all I had to deal with was the dirty feeling it left on my soul. That, at least, was familiar. Perhaps I'd even grow numb to it over time. My parents had.

I'd call Tom McClanahan once I made it home and tell him to give Sugarwood to whoever he felt would best manage it and support the community. At least that way I wasn't hurting anyone.

I climbed into my car and headed for Fay's house. She was the last one I still needed to say goodbye to before I left, and I wanted to do it in person. I'd tried to call Mark, but since I hadn't answered or returned any of his calls over the past few days, it seemed he now wouldn't answer mine. I'd left him a voicemail instead.

Chief Wilson's cruiser wasn't in the driveway when I pulled in. I dialed Fay's cell phone to see if she wanted me to come in rather than making her answer the door, but her phone rang until it went to voicemail.

I headed for the door and rang the bell. The neighborhood seemed quiet this time of day. A few birds chittering at each other in the trees and the drone of a leaf blower a block or two over were the only sounds.

After two minutes, I tried the bell again.

No answer.

My heart accelerated. I dialed her cell a second time. It was possible she wasn't home. I might be panicking over nothing.

Inside the house, not too far from the door, came Fay's distinctive ringtone, the one I'd teased her about sounding like amorous robots.

It felt like someone stomped on my chest, sharp and heavy and painful. I tried the door handle. The door was unlocked.

I pulled it open. "Fay?"

My voice echoed back to me from the vaulted entryway. I inched the door open.

The living room lay directly across from the entryway, and my mind seemed to only be able to process a single detail at a time.

The bowl and bottle of some blue drink sitting on the coffee table. Fay's cell phone on the floor. Fay's hand hanging limp above it. Fay on the sofa.

The world snapped back into real time and I dashed across the house, yelling her name. It must have been me yelling. There was no one else there, but it didn't seem like it came from me.

She still had a pulse, but I couldn't tell if she was breathing. Surely she had to still be breathing. She didn't seem to be breathing.

I dialed 9-1-1, put the phone on speaker, and tore off my sling and started CPR. My injured shoulder felt like someone stabbed it with a thousand knives, but I refused to stop.

Everything between then and climbing into my car to follow the ambulance to the hospital blurred together. I only remember stuffing Fay's phone into her purse and taking it with me, thinking she might have an insurance card or some other information in her wallet that they'd need.

I hit redial, redial, redial on Fay's phone, trying to reach Chief Wilson, but he didn't answer. What kind of a husband didn't answer every call his sick wife made to him? Then again, I didn't know if he was interviewing a suspect in a crime or out in the field. Rationally I knew I shouldn't judge him so harshly, but he should be here for her, not me. I couldn't make any decisions. The doctors wouldn't even share her condition with me once we got there. I'd be stuck waiting without any sense of how she was. Stupid privacy laws.

I followed the stretcher through the hospital doors and as far down the hall as they'd let me. When a nurse directed me to the waiting room, I just stood there. Because I couldn't continue home now and I couldn't sit here, either. If I sat here, it'd be admitting that Fay wasn't going to make it. I had to do something in the hope that she was.

I headed back the way I'd come, my purse over one shoulder and Fay's over the other. I'd swing by the police station and see if Chief Wilson was there. Then I'd go by Fay's house and put a bag together for her. When my friend Ahanti broke her leg skiing and had to stay in the hospital, she'd had me do that for her. Ahanti insisted that having a few of your own things, even fresh socks, could make a stay in the hospital bearable. Fay's stay might be a long one, and I couldn't stand the thought of her with cold feet or forced to wear the same socks for a week or more.

The woman working the front desk at the police station told me Chief Wilson wasn't in. I gave her my name.

"He knows me. I'm a friend of his wife's." As well as a pain in his rear prior to this point, but *friend of his wife* was more likely to get me the results I wanted. "Fay was taken by ambulance to the hospital, and I can't get ahold of him. I was hoping you could contact him."

The woman swore. "Yeah, I'll call him on his radio right away."

Some of the weight that'd been dragging down on my shoulders since I found Fay eased. "Could you also let him know that I'm headed back to their house to pick up some of her things? I don't want him worrying about any of that."

The woman nodded. She was already putting out the call.

I jogged back to my car. My cell phone rang. I thought about ignoring it, but it might be Chief Wilson.

I awkwardly fished it out while sliding into the driver's seat and buckling in. "Hello?"

"Nikki," Russ said. "Please don't hang up."

That's exactly what I wanted to do. I should have checked my caller ID. I'd had quite enough of lies and betrayal, thank you very much. I didn't need this now. "How are you even calling me?"

"I'm out on bail. I didn't kill Stan, and I didn't try to hurt you. You have to believe me."

I switched the call to the speakers in my car and pulled out onto the road. "I don't actually. Goodbye, Russ."

"Please. It's important. I didn't do this, and that means the real killer is still out there."

Yes, Virginia, and there is a Santa Claus. "I'm going to hang up now. I don't have time for this. Fay is in the hospital."

Russ's sharp intake of breath came through the phone as loudly as if he stood beside me. "Is she alright? What happened?"

He sounded panicked. Honest to goodness, freaked out, I-misplaced-$100,000 panicked. My throat spasmed shut.

Russ' friend with the one bottle of Beaver's Tail Beer. The beer that no local drank. And nowhere in Jason's brewery did he have single bottles for sale. Only six packs. The one bottle in Fay's fridge, leftovers from Chief Wilson's tests. All of them the same type of beer.

I might be about to make a huge fool of myself, but I didn't think so. "Is Fay the women you were having an affair with?"

The silence on his end spoke the truth louder than words. "How long?"

"Six months. I was even the one going with her to most of her doctor's appointments. Carl never had the time to take her."

The nicest way to describe Russ was homely, but setting aside the fact that he was currently under arrest for murdering my uncle, I could see what a woman whose husband seemed to care more about his job than about her would see in Russ. From the moment I'd met him, he'd shown a tendency to make choices that put others' comfort above his own and to be there when you needed him.

I turned into Fay's driveway and leaned my head back against the headrest. Did I really believe that kind of a man would kill someone over a business, no matter how much he loved it? But if not him, then who? It felt like I was missing the all-important connection that would help this make sense.

I disconnected the phone from the car and went into the house. "Did Chief Wilson know about the affair?"

Russ gave a little humph, the equivalent of a verbal shrug. "Not that I know of. Fay could dye her hair purple and he probably wouldn't notice."

I think Russ underestimated him. A man didn't rise to Chief Wilson's position in life, and spend that many years investigating crimes, without being observant. But if he had found out, that would give him motive to murder Russ or Fay, but not Uncle Stan.

Holy crap! I stopped in my tracks halfway to the stairs.

"Holy crap what?" Russ said.

I hadn't realized that'd been out loud. "Give me a minute. I'm thinking." What if Fay was the intended victim and Uncle Stan figured it out? "How long before Uncle Stan died did he start looking into Fay's heart condition?"

"I'm not sure exactly. Maybe a couple of days."

"Okay, so stick with me on this because it's going to sound crazy at first. If someone wanted to mimic heart problems to set up a murder, how would they do it?"

A beat of silence. "I don't know. But the whole issue with Jason Wood was over the caffeine in his beer and Stan thinking it could have hurt my heart."

Caffeine. Of course. That's why Uncle Stan had the book beside his bed open to caffeine's interactions with the heart. In retrospect, I'd thought he'd probably been looking into it because of the situation with Jason and the beer, but that was over long enough ago that Uncle Stan should have put the book back on his shelf. He was meticulous about that. The only books he ever left out were the ones he was currently reading.

After examining Fay, he must have guessed her heart condition wasn't natural. He'd gone looking for the most likely cause. And Chief Wilson had to know it was only a matter of time before Stan started talking to Fay about environmental factors or someone trying to intentionally hurt her.

"I think Chief Wilson was poisoning Fay and he killed Uncle Stan to keep him from figuring it out. I'm in their house now, so I'm going to take a quick peek and see if I can spot anything that might prove—"

Something cold and round pressed against the back of my neck.

Russ was still talking in my ear. "I don't think that's wise, Nikki. You need to call it in. Or if you don't trust the police, call Mark."

His words only registered peripherally. A heavy hand on my shoulder turned me around slowly until I faced the gun. And the man holding it.

Chapter 21

"Say goodbye," Chief Wilson whispered.

And for a crazy second I wasn't sure if he wanted me to casually say goodbye to the person on the phone or if he was saying he was about to put a bullet into my brain like a TV mobster. But obviously he wasn't going to shoot me with Russ on the phone as a witness. Not after what he'd heard me say.

"And tell him you've decided to head home after all," he whispered again. "This town isn't safe."

It certainly wasn't, I wanted to say. But my mouth complied. "I've got to go, Russ. You're right. I'm supposed to be heading home anyway."

"Nikki, wa—"

I disconnected the call.

Chief Wilson lowered the gun slightly, but kept it pointed at me. "Put the phone in your pocket and keep your hands in plain sight."

My brain slowly ticked over to an unnatural calm. I'd expected a fresh panic attack. Or maybe nausea. I could imagine myself barfing all over Chief Wilson's shoes. But none of that happened. "I'm guessing you heard most of that conversation?"

"The parts since you came into the house."

The crazy-calm part of my brain said to keep him talking because as long as he was talking, he wasn't shooting. "Where's your car?"

"Parked a few streets away. I didn't want anyone wondering why I was here after I got the call about my sick wife. And my dispatcher said you'd also be coming here. I couldn't have you getting suspicious."

Obviously he hadn't thought to use the excuse that he came here to pick up some personal items for her. Maybe that's something only a woman would think to do. Or maybe that would have made the staff at the hospital suspicious, because wouldn't a devoted husband want to stay as close to his wife as possible when her life was at risk? Or maybe he knew his dispatcher would question if he'd been here when she knew I was here.

Regardless, there could be only one reason he came back here after receiving the news about Fay. "You were going to wait until I was gone and then get rid of the evidence."

"I know how quickly an investigation can progress if someone decided one was needed. I wasn't taking a chance. And I guess it's a good thing I didn't."

I didn't want to ask what he planned to do with me and bring his attention back to the fact that I'd become a liability. I needed to keep him talking until I could figure out how to escape. What I wouldn't give for a steak knife right about now. "How did you find out? About the affair I mean."

He motioned with the gun that I should move toward the back door. "Storm over the summer knocked out our power. I couldn't find my phone in the dark to call the power company and check in with the office. So I used Fay's. And saw a text come in from Russ making sure she was alright, was I home, did she need him to come over."

Nothing explicit, but Chief Wilson wasn't a stupid man, either. The planning he seemed to have put into all this proved as much. "I guess you followed her after that."

I was reaching for conversational straws, but nothing I passed as I edged slowly backward would work as a weapon or a means of escape. A couch pillow wasn't going to stop a bullet. Throwing it at him also wasn't likely to distract him long enough for me to escape. The man was a trained law enforcement officer.

"Followed her and confirmed my suspicions. Twenty years we've been married and she chooses to prostitute herself out like I haven't given her a better life than anyone else in this town has."

"Why not divorce her? It didn't have to end up like this for anyone."

"I'm up for election as sheriff next year." Chief Wilson cringed. "As soon as it came out that my wife left me for Russell Dantry, I'd be a laughingstock and no one in the county would vote for me. I'm not going to be stuck running the tiny municipal police department in this town until I die."

My dad always said that greed was a stronger motivator than love. I wanted to crack Chief Wilson in the nose for no other reason than adding proof to my father's theory.

We were almost to the door. Could I somehow pat my pocket in such a way that my phone would dial? Not likely. It'd been long enough that I'd have to put the passcode back in.

He pointed to the left. "Not that way. Go left, into the garage."

That wasn't good. He probably didn't intend to shoot me after all. He was too smart for that. Too much noise. Too much chance of a neighbor hearing it and calling it in. But he could have any manner of things in the garage that would kill me quietly.

I stopped. Time for a different tactic. "I can see why you'd be angry. You've given her everything she should want, right? A nice house. Security."

Chief Wilson laughed, and it sounded a bit like a lawnmower struggling to start. "That's not going to work on me, Ms. Fitzhenry-Dawes." He slurred my last name again. "I know the tricks of the trade."

No more subterfuge then. I wished I could cross my arms to give the impression of calm and strength, but my injured shoulder ached from the CPR I'd done on Fay. I wasn't sure I could lift it even that far. "So what do you plan to do with me? People will wonder where I went."

"I doubt it. Haven't you been telling the whole town goodbye? It'll look like you headed home. And if you don't make it, your family will assume something happened to you along the way."

Arg. He was probably right.

Which meant I had no reason to go into that garage. I had no reason to do anything he said.

If he wanted to kill me, I was going to make him do it the hard way. The hard, loud, attention-drawing, guilty-finger pointing way.

Chapter 22

The lessons from my self-defense classes flooded into my brain in a jumbled mess. Panic scrabbled at my throat, making it hard to breathe. I was only supposed to have to defend myself and draw enough attention to attract help. Attacking first was never part of the training.

But some things still applied. Chief Wilson was stronger and better trained. My only hope was to aim for a vulnerable spot and scratch like crazy to get his DNA under my fingernails. I might not survive this, but I was going to leave as much evidence for the police and prosecutor as possible.

The most vulnerable spot on a man was his groin, and if any man deserved an elbow in the nuts, it was him.

I let out a screech that I hoped would both throw him off and draw the attention of every neighbor on the block, ducked low, and launched myself toward his lower half.

I missed my target and smashed good shoulder first into his stomach instead.

The gun boomed somewhere above my head, and we hurtled backward. One of his limbs clipped me in the chin, sending hot darts through my face, and the warm copper tang of blood flooded my mouth. Black twirled across my vision.

We tumbled into the side of the recliner. It tipped and crashed backward.

As I went down, I caught a glimpse of the front door. It didn't seem as far away as it had before. If he'd lost his grip on the gun in the fall, I might be able to make it. I scrambled forward on hands and knees.

A hand clamped around my ankle and yanked me back. I flopped onto my belly like a land-bound fish. For a second, all I could think was that this was not a very graceful way to die, which, sadly enough, was fitting, since I'd never been very graceful in life.

Chief Wilson planted a knee into the small of my back and wrapped a large hand around the side of my head. He crushed my face into the cold wood floor.

"You can't ever do what you're told, can you?" His words came out in a snarl.

"Not when what I'm being told is wrong." It was difficult to speak with my face all flattened, but the extra hard squeeze he gave my head gave away that he'd understood me.

"I didn't want to have to hurt you."

The front door slammed back against the wall. "Let her go."

Russ!

Even though Chief Wilson kept me firmly trapped, I recognized Russ' voice. When I disconnected our call, he must have jumped into his truck and driven straight here.

Chief Wilson's weight on my back shifted slightly. "Go home, Russ. If you don't, I'll snap her neck and blame it on you. It'll be your word against mine, and who do you think people will believe?"

"I always knew you had an ego bigger than your heart," Russ said. "I'm not leaving her here with you."

I had to assume Chief Wilson had lost his gun in our tussle. Otherwise he would have threatened to shoot me or to shoot Russ. If Russ could grab it, we might still make it out of here. "He dropped his gun—"

The crushing weight vanished from my back. I rolled to the side in time to see Chief Wilson dive for the gun and Russ dive for Chief Wilson. They went down in a tangle of limbs.

Russ might be strong from the physical labor involved with working the maple bush, but no way was he going to be a match for a police officer in hand-to-hand combat.

I fished for my phone, but stopped before I reached it. Calling for help wouldn't be fast enough. He could shoot us both before the 9-1-1 dispatcher even answered and blame it on Russ.

I stumbled to my feet and grabbed a lamp from the end table. The shade toppled off, and a light tug signaled the cord popping from the wall. I sprinted toward the fight.

I'd always been terrible at sports, baseball included, but Chief Wilson's head made a much bigger target than a baseball. Even I couldn't miss it.

I swung the lamp and the base cracked him in the skull, above his ear.

He dropped to his knees. Russ wrenched the gun from his grip and turned it on Chief Wilson.

I skittered around the couch to stand beside Russ. Wilson rubbed the back of his head, a dazed look on his face.

"I know I'm not your uncle and you're a grown woman," Russ said, "but I'm not asking this time. I'm telling you. Call the police."

I set down the lamp and did as I was told.

For what seemed like hours, the police questioned Russ and me separately, then sent in an EMT to check me over and put my arm back in a sling.

I couldn't tell exactly how long it took or what time it was because my watch had broken during the fight, they took my cell phone, and apparently no one thought a clock was necessary in the room they tucked me in to. This must be some form of psychological trick to put pressure on suspects.

Sometime after I started pacing the floor, a balding officer brought Russ in.

The officer nodded at me. "Shouldn't be long now, miss."

Russ sank heavily into the nearest chair. It creaked under his weight.

I dragged another chair over beside him. "Do you think this means they've decided we're telling the truth?"

"I guess so." He glanced at the door. "I passed the county sheriff and two of his deputies on the way here. They wouldn't have brought in someone from the outside if they weren't taking this seriously and considering charging Carl."

His voice had a hollow edge to it, and his shoulders slumped forward. I would have wondered why he didn't look happier over being proven innocent if it wasn't for the fact that I knew how he felt about Fay.

"Would they tell you anything about Fay?"

I knew he must have asked. I'd asked both the officers who questioned me. They either didn't know anything or wouldn't tell me. They hadn't given me a reason for their refusal. I'd briefly considered requesting that they let me see Erik, but I didn't want to put him in a bad position.

"Quincey,"—Russ waved his hand toward the door, and I guessed he meant the officer who brought him to my room—"said it didn't look good. They've had to put her on life support, and they're running scans to see if there's any brain activity."

An ache built in my stomach. It'd been one thing to know she might die because of a problem with her heart that was outside of anyone's control, but it was something else completely to think about her hooked up to machines and dying because the man who should have loved and protected her hurt her instead.

"She was with me because she was lonely." Russ rocked back and forth in his chair, back and forth. "I was with her because I loved her. I should have listened to Stan when he told me to break it off. He told me sleeping with a married woman would bring trouble and pain. But she didn't want to give Carl up, and I didn't want to lose her. Even though I knew Stan was right and what I was doing was wrong."

Any response I could come up with felt callous. Callous, and then there was that old saying about people in glass houses. If I hadn't wanted to keep my ex so badly, I would have noticed the signs that said he was

married. But I didn't want to see. I didn't want to face
the truth. And then I couldn't see it.

It seemed to be a pattern with me, one that I wasn't
proud of. "I'm sorry I didn't believe you when you said
you'd never hurt Uncle Stan. Maybe if I had—"

He clamped his hand over mine. "This isn't your
fault. Don't even go there."

He was right, but it didn't feel that way. I'd assumed he was lying because I'd been lied to before.
And it turned out blind disbelief wasn't any better a
way to live than blind belief had been. Maybe the best
path was somewhere in the middle, where trust and
cynicism met up to form common sense.

"I'm sorry anyway." I patted the top of our joined
hands. "Thank you for coming to my rescue."

He smiled even though it had a sad edge to it. "I was
doing what your uncle would've done if he were still
here."

We sat for a few minutes in silence, sharing the
grief that we couldn't share in words. Words couldn't
bring back the people we'd lost, but I could put one
thing right. "I was thinking that owning Sugarwood
might be too much for me."

Russ' gaze snapped to my face, and he frowned.
"You're not planning on selling the place? So many
people depend on—"

I held my palm out toward him in the universal sign
for *wait*. "That it might be too much for me on my

own. I was thinking of taking on a partner, and I was hoping you might be interested in the job."

Chapter 23

I stayed over in Fair Haven for Fay's funeral. I hadn't known her long, but I'd counted her a friend, and I wanted a chance to say a final good-bye.

As the funeral broke up, Mark approached me, his shoulders hunched against the wind.

He scrubbed a hand over his hair and looked past my face rather than meeting my gaze. "Russ said you were planning to leave right after the funeral, but do you have time for a quick walk with me first?"

It was late enough in the day that I'd have to find a hotel somewhere halfway anyway, so a few more minutes wouldn't matter. I motioned toward the sugar maple bush butting up against the cemetery. "Let's get out of the wind at least."

A wide path marked by poles at five-foot intervals blocked a path out from the bush around it, cultivation in the midst of the wild. The path allowed us to walk side by side.

"I owe you an apology," Mark said.

I rubbed my hands up my arms, trying to generate some extra warmth. "For what?"

"I didn't take your call the day Fay died. I feel like—"

I waved my hand as if I could brush his apology away. "It wouldn't have made a difference. It wasn't until I was talking to Russ that I put things together. You couldn't have known Carl Wilson would be in the house when I showed up. And besides, I hadn't answered your calls for days either."

"Still."

The silence settled over us, broken only by the trees' bare branches clattering together overhead and the crunch of decaying leaves underfoot.

"Will this go to trial?" I asked.

I had plenty of experience sitting in courtrooms, both observing and serving as junior counsel, but I'd never had to go as a witness. If Wilson—I couldn't call him *Chief* anymore—decided to take his chances, I couldn't see any way I'd be exempt from testifying.

Mark shook his head. "He took a plea deal. He knew he'd never survive in the general population as a former police chief. In exchange for solitary, he admitted to everything."

I drew my first deep breath in what felt like a solid week. The near-winter air bit my lungs, but it also made me feel sharp and vibrant. I wanted to breathe it in this time rather than hiding from it the way I had when I first came to Fair Haven. Maybe I'd make a Michigan girl after all.

"He told me why he did it." I stopped, pulled off a mitt, and ran my fingers along the ropy ridges of the nearest sugar maple tree. My sugar maple tree. In a few months, Russ and the others would be collecting sap from them, and I'd be learning a new skill. "What I'm still curious about is how? You can tell me that right, since it'll be public record?"

Mark stepped in close, looking down at me. His gaze dipped to my lips and my breath caught.

He pulled a leaf fragment from my hair and stepped back. "Apparently he knew about Fay's affair for a while, and he was waiting until he could find a good way to murder her without getting caught."

"And when Uncle Stan made a fuss about the caffeine content in Beaver's Tail beer and how dangerous it could be to a healthy heart..." I was guessing, but it sounded reasonable.

"Mmhmm," Mark said. "He used the investigation into Jason Wood and Beaver's Tail Brewery to get what he needed. He took an extra canister of the caffeine powder Jason uses in his beer, but never entered it into evidence, so there'd be no record of him buying caffeine powder. Then he bought his own six-packs of the beer itself in the name of testing it for the investigation. What he was actually trying to figure out was how high a dosage he needed to use in order to either cause or mimic heart problems. He didn't want to leave an online trail by searching for the information that way."

The rest of how it happened all lined up like dominoes. Fay got sick, and her doctors couldn't understand why her seemingly healthy heart was showings symptoms of distress. When Fay learned about Uncle Stan's past career and he offered to help, Uncle Stan became a threat to Wilson's plan.

"Did he say how..." My throat closed and it took me a minute to take control again. "My Uncle Stan. How did it happen?"

Mark's hand reached toward me like he wanted to offer comfort, then dropped back to his side. We were in such an awkward no man's land. He was married, and aside from the relationship I was beginning to explore with Erik, I refused to be the other woman. Hopefully, though, Mark and I could find a way to be friends without all the awkwardness.

The wind blew his hair over his forehead, and he brushed it back. "Stan told Fay about his own heart, so Carl knew. He showed up at Stan's house unexpectedly and forced him to overdose. The way Carl tells it, he said it was either that or he'd kill Russ as well."

It made sense. Uncle Stan wouldn't have been any more likely than I would to go easily and do what he was told. If he was going to die, he would have wanted to make it clear he was murdered. Carl Wilson pressed the only button that would have made Uncle Stan comply—he'd threatened to hurt someone my uncle cared about.

"What was his endgame with Fay?" I asked.

"Once he'd used the high doses of caffeine for long enough to establish a pre-existing heart condition, he planned to poison her with antifreeze. You found her when she'd finally taken in a lethal amount."

I'd heard of dogs and cats and raccoons dying from drinking antifreeze, something about it tasting sweet. It seemed like an ignoble way for such a lovely woman to die. "How did he get her to drink it without her knowing?"

"The techs found it in a few different items in their fridge. Carl would have known which ones to avoid, and Fay would have slowly been killing herself."

"But wouldn't the doctors have known? Surely antifreeze poisoning couldn't have been considered accidental."

"He wasn't aiming for accidental. Her death would have been ruled a heart attack. Her body would have metabolized the antifreeze, so unless we had a reason after her death to check for high amounts of calcium oxalate crystals in her tissues, a byproduct of the metabolism of antifreeze, no one would have suspected she was poisoned. Deaths from antifreeze poisoning often present as undetermined, and so the doctors will logically default to listing cause of death based on a prior health issue if there's one on record."

Since Fay's heart problems were well known by now, that would have been the official cause listed, and no one would have looked for anything further.

I marched off at a pace that might have been a little too brisk. Wilson's plan was premeditated murder at its height. He'd thought it through carefully, and he'd watched his wife slowly die. The unmerciful part of me wished he hadn't made a plea and had found himself in the general population, where cops had a short life expectancy. Apparently mercy wasn't one of my strengths, either.

Fay might have broken her marriage vows, but she didn't deserve to die.

Mark grabbed my arm and drew me to a halt. I could feel the warmth of his hand through my jacket. My heart tugged in two directions, one warmed by Mark's touch and the other by the care shown by Erik's scarf and mittens.

"You did a good thing," Mark said. "If you hadn't come here, insisting someone killed your uncle, Carl would have gotten away with it all. I hope you'll reconsider staying."

I slipped out of his grip, continuing on the path back to my car a little more slowly now. I couldn't bring Fay or Uncle Stan back, but Wilson wouldn't hurt anyone else, and Russ wouldn't be going to prison for something he didn't do.

Maybe I couldn't make the world just or fair, but I didn't have to spend my life working to put the guilty back out into the world in the name of due process, either. It was time to figure out what I wanted from my life and how I could make a positive difference.

"I have to go back."

Mark's expression fell.

"But only to pack up my belongings and sub-let my apartment," I said. "I'll hopefully be back here before Christmas. If my first couple of weeks in Fair Haven are any indication, I certainly won't be bored living here."

"Just wait," Mark said with a grin. "It isn't even tourist season yet."

Maple-Glazed Pork ala Russ

INGREDIENTS:

2 1/2 pounds boneless pork loin roast
1 cup real maple syrup
4 tablespoons Dijon mustard
2 1/2 tablespoons apple cider vinegar
2 1/2 tablespoons soy sauce
1/4 teaspoon salt
1/8 teaspoon pepper

INSTRUCTIONS:

1. Preheat the oven to 375 degrees F (190 degrees C).
2. Mix together all the ingredients (except the pork loin, of course).

3. Place the pork loin roast in a shallow roasting pan. Pour the glaze over the pork. Make sure it's completely coated.

4. Roast pork in the oven uncovered for about 1 hour or until a meat thermometer reaches the correct temperature for your desired doneness. Baste pork with glaze 2-3 times during roasting.

5. Remove from oven and let rest 5-10 minutes before serving.

6. If desired, you can serve the sauce from the pan alongside the meat.

SERVES 8 people (or one person with lots of leftovers like Russ).

LETTER FROM THE AUTHOR

Thank you so much for going on this journey alongside Nicole. I had so much fun writing this book, and I hope you had fun reading it. I have many more adventures in store for Nicole, Mark, Erik, and the others.

The second book in the series, *Bushwhacked*, is already available in print, ebook, and audio versions. If you'd like to know as soon as future books release, sign up for my newsletter at www.smarturl.it/emilyjames.

As a thank you gift for signing up, you'll also receive an ebook copy of the prequel, *Sapped*. In this novella, I reveal what happened to sour Nicole on being a lawyer and make her wary of married men.

If you enjoyed *A Sticky Inheritance*, I'd really appreciate it if you also took a minute to write a quick review wherever you bought the book. Reviews help me sell more books (which allows me to keep writing them), and they also help fellow readers know if this is a book they might enjoy.

ABOUT THE AUTHOR

Emily James grew up watching TV shows like *Matlock*, *Monk*, and *Murder She Wrote*. (It's pure coincidence that they all begin with an **M**.) It was no surprise to anyone when she turned into a mystery writer.

Alongside being a writer, she's also a wife, an animal lover, and a new artist. She likes coffee and painting and drinking coffee while painting. She also enjoys cooking. She tries not to do that while painting because, well, you shouldn't eat paint.

Emily and her husband share their home with a blue Great Dane, seven cats (all rescues), and a budgie (who is both the littlest and the loudest).
If you'd like to know as soon as Emily's next mystery releases, please join her newsletter list at www.smarturl.it/emilyjames.

She also loves hearing from readers. You can email her through her website (www.authoremilyjames.com) or find her on Facebook (www.facebook.com/authoremilyjames/).

Made in the USA
Las Vegas, NV
27 November 2024

12763585R00146